Bushpig

By

Carol Preston

WESTVIEW BOOK PUBLISHING, INC., NASHVILLE, TENNESSEE

ISBN 1-933912-70-7

Printed in the United States of America on acid-free paper.

First Edition, April 2007

Cover design by Hugh Daniel

Page Layout by Mary Catharine Nelson

Edited by Bob Allen and Judy Allen, Author's, Corner, LLC.

Author Representative: Bob Allen, Author's Corner, LLC

WESTVIEW BOOK PUBLISHING, INC.
P.O. Box 210183
Nashville, Tennessee 37221
www.westviewpublishing.com

Dedication

This book is dedicated to my husband, without whom I could not imagine pushing myself to the limits that it takes to write this story. I also wish to honor my friends and family who gave me encouragement while I struggled with the notion of trying to get published.

Disclaimer

This is a work of fiction. Any similarity to any person living or dead is co-incidental and not intended. Any similarity to any location is also co-incidental and not intended.

Prologue

"So, how do you handle stress?" the woman asked, leaning across the table toward me. She looked arrogant as she stared a hole in me waiting for an answer. I always thought it was amusing to see someone act so superior in an interview just because they sit on one side of a desk and you're sitting on the other trying to prove yourself worthy of a job.

I leaned in closer to her, looked her straight in the eye and answered, "Well, I buried my mother this morning. How do you think I handle stress?"

The woman sat back in her chair and adjusted her jacket. I couldn't tell how she felt about what I said, but at that point I really didn't care anyway. As she sat there and let my words sink in for a moment, I wondered how she could have even asked such a stupid question.

My mother's funeral had been that morning, and because I needed that job so badly, I was willing to go to the interview even though I was not mentally capable of going through the charade of acting like a smart, competent candidate. I had tried to get another appointment time for the interview and even explained to the company's recruiter that this was not a good day and the reason why it wasn't. Her reply was, "This is the only day we have available to meet with you. It's between you and another candidate. Do you think you can make it?" It's almost like she didn't hear what I had said at all.

The damnedest thing of all is that I didn't even get the job.

So, how do you handle stress? That's a question you will be asking yourself as you read this book. When do you walk away from a bad situation and when do you dig your heels into the ground, push up your sleeves, and hit it straight on with everything you've got? What if you can't walk away? What if you want to kick your own ass for making a big mess of your life?

Bushpig is a story about a couple who purchases an historic house to renovate while they're in the midst of coping with several personal issues. Somehow they believe that it will be the common ground that repairs their crumbling relationship.

As the story unfolds, not only does the couple manage the enormous task of remodeling a house that should've been demolished, they also have financial difficulties, marriage troubles, neighbor problems, and they are dealing with the death of a family member. As a result, their lives are turned upside down with stress and grief. They get to the point of madness at times, trying to handle everything that they've brought onto themselves.

This story provides a fascinating view into the main characters' transformation from being an optimistic, caring couple to tired, cynical versions of themselves as they struggle to get through an unfortunate set of circumstances.

So sit back and allow yourself to imagine being in the same situation. How much self control could you have in similar conditions? How close to the edge can you be pushed?

Bushpig

Chapter 1

Suzanne walked toward the hospital with her shirt sticking to her back. It was August, and the heat was unrelenting. The hot weather and the concern she had for her sick mother left her feeling tired and discouraged. She trudged across the parking lot with a bag of magazines for her mother. Suzanne had a bad feeling about her mother's health and the way the doctors provided only vague explanations of her prognosis and little, if any, encouraging remarks. Suzanne hadn't asked them many direct questions about her mother; she had trusted that the doctors or nurses would tell her what she needed to know. At this point, however, it seemed they weren't even sure what was wrong. Several tests had been taken with no clear answers. Suzanne was feeling impatient with the doctors and wanted more information.

When Suzanne got to the hospital room, her mother was looking stronger than she had in several days. She was sitting up in bed and had the food tray in front of her with a few bites taken from a piece of cake. Her eyes looked clear and bright, and her breathing didn't seem to be as labored as it had been. Suzanne's uncle was in the room with her mother when she got there.

"Hey, Mama, you sure do look better today!" Suzanne said with a smile as she entered the room.

Suzanne's Uncle David stood from the chair in the corner of the hospital room and walked over to hug Suzanne. "Hey, girl, it's good to see you," he said as he gave her a squeeze.

"It's so hot outside; I thought I'd melt before I could get in here!" Suzanne teased. "Mama, how are you feeling?"

"I feel a little better today. The doctor said I could probably go home this weekend," Ruth said as she adjusted her gown around her shoulders. She still looked fragile, but she had a look of determination Suzanne hadn't seen in her for weeks.

"I told her she needs to eat," Uncle David said and winked at Suzanne's mother. "She needs to move those legs, too, 'cause she hasn't walked in weeks." He shook his finger at Ruth. "You can't go home until you get up and walk. So, wiggle those legs and eat."

Ruth laughed. "Yeah, I know it. You'll keep me straight, huh, David?" She carefully shifted her weight onto her other side.

Suzanne knew how much her mother loved Uncle David, and she was grateful that he had come to spend time at her bedside. If only he could get her to move around a little. Ruth had been bedridden for several days at this point and hadn't been able to even get up and go to the bathroom by herself yet. It worried Suzanne that her mother's health had not improved since being in the hospital.

Suzanne went to the side of the bed and took hold of Ruth's calf, slowly and gently bending her leg. "Does that hurt, Mama?" Suzanne asked.

"Not really. Actually, it feels pretty good," Ruth said optimistically. She was smiling a little, and Suzanne felt relieved that her mother didn't seem to be in a lot of pain.

The nurse who came in to check the monitor was hinting with her eyes that it was time for them to leave. Suzanne was frustrated with the short visiting hours of the intensive care unit. It took so long to get to the hospital and back home, just to see her mother for a few minutes.

Uncle David and Suzanne walked toward the door. "We're going to have to leave now, but I'm coming back tomorrow. You look really good. Try to eat, okay?" Suzanne said as she bent down to kiss her mother goodbye.

Ruth softly patted Suzanne on the arm and said, "I will." She laid her head back against her pillow and closed her eyes. "I think I'm going to try to get some sleep. Those nurses come in here all hours of the night waking me up. A person can't get any rest in a hospital."

"How do you think she looks?" Suzanne asked her uncle when they got out into the hallway.

"I think she looks better than she did yesterday, that's for sure. Your mama says the doctor might let her go home in a few days. Maybe whatever's been making her so sick is finally going to get better with all of this medicine she's been taking." Uncle David put his hands in his pockets and looked at the floor.

"I hope you're right."

"When Ruth gets home, somebody's going to have to take care of her."

"I've been thinking about that. You know, Elaine lives right behind her," Suzanne answered.

"Your sister is as busy as you are, ain't she?"

"Yeah, but Daddy's there, too. And I can help on the weekends. If we all take some time to watch after Mama, she should be fine. She's not crazy about anybody doing things for her, but she really doesn't have a choice."

"Well, if you need some help getting her home and settled when they release her, give me a call and I'll come drive her back to the house."

"I appreciate that. Yes, I'll let you know if we need help."

"Alright, then. I'll see you tomorrow, Honey."

Suzanne left the hospital feeling better about her mother and thinking about how different things will be when she comes home. It was an overwhelming thought, and Suzanne decided to talk about it with her husband over dinner. They were separated, but they were still very close and saw each other almost every day.

"Mama looks good," Suzanne told Jerry when they sat down at the restaurant. "She still looks pretty weak, but she's breathing better, and she really wants to come home."

"Well, that's good news. What are the doctors saying?"

"From what I understand, they think her pneumonia is gone, but they'll do more tests before they release her from the hospital, I'm sure. The only thing that concerns me, Jerry, is that she still hasn't been able to get up and walk yet. How can she go home if she can't even get around the hospital room?"

Jerry set down the menu and took off his reading glasses. "Oh, she's going to be fine. Your mom is tough. The doctors won't let her go home until she's ready. Besides, there's nothing wrong with her legs. If she really is over the pneumonia, then she'll be getting her strength back soon." Jerry's encouragement seemed to come with some effort, but his support was reassuring.

Suzanne studied Jerry's face as he spoke. He was still a good-looking man at age forty-six. His dark skin complimented his black hair and brown eyes. The gray streaks in his hair gave him a mature look, as did the reading glasses he often wore. When Jerry laughed, his whole face gave in to a big toothy grin. Suzanne was glad that they had remained friends despite their separation.

When the waitress came over to the table, they ordered their food. Since they were both tired, they ate mostly in silence, each in their own world of thought. Suzanne's mind was still on her mother.

After Suzanne got back to her apartment, she thought about Jerry as she brushed her teeth and got ready for bed. It was too quiet without him and she longed for a friend to talk to. I could call him, she thought. Instead, she went to bed and tried not to dwell on the loneliness that she felt since she'd moved out on her own several months ago when they separated.

Suzanne thought about the constant bitterness Jerry carried around when he couldn't find work. That, coupled with the fact that he was eighteen years older than her, made him seem more like a grumpy old man than a lover. As time went on, she realized that she cared for him deeply, but she wasn't in love with him anymore.

As she turned out the lights and lay in bed alone that night, she wondered if being in love was so important anyway. She wished he was there with her to keep her company while she thought about her mother.

For the next few days Ruth's condition stayed about the same. The doctor didn't release her as she had hoped. He thought she still might be susceptible to pneumonia and wanted to keep her hospitalized to make sure her breathing continued to stabilize, and hopefully improve.

Suzanne visited her mother as much as possible and called the hospital every day to check on her progress. She stayed in touch with her father and sister for updates since they lived closer to the hospital and were able to visit her every day.

Chapter 2

"**I** think I found a house for us," Suzanne said when Jerry answered the phone.

"Wait a minute . . . what did you say, a house? Where is it?" Jerry asked. He wiped his hands on a towel next to the phone. He was washing dishes when it rang.

"It's on Cumberland Street, off Glenview Avenue," Suzanne explained. "The realtor told me it needed updating, but it's in an historic neighborhood and it's a very good price."

Jerry knew that Suzanne had been looking for a place to buy, but he thought she wanted to live on her own. He was surprised that she was including him in her plans, but played along to see where she was going with this.

"That's over there where William lives," said Jerry. William was a friend of Jerry's with whom he played basketball. "Have you gone to look at it yet?"

"Not yet, but I'd like to. If you're not too busy right now, I'll come over there and pick you up, then we can ride over together and take a look."

"I guess so. Come on by, I'll be here," Jerry said and hung up the phone. He never knew what to expect from Suzanne these days.

Jerry and Suzanne pulled up in front of the house at 2010 Cumberland Street with anticipation. The house was fairly handsome, although it had green aluminum siding and obviously needed work. The porch had a distinct lean and the bungalow-style porch posts were settling to the point that the roofline was sagging. There was a small front yard that sloped downhill toward the right side of the house. On either side of the house were two other historic homes.

They got out of Suzanne's truck and walked up the front steps of the walkway toward the house. Jerry glanced at the house situated to the left. It was a little hard to make out because of the overgrown trees and bushes around it, but Jerry could see that it wasn't very well kept. On the porch were some broken-down bookshelves, a couple of rusty metal chairs, and an old refrigerator. In the yard, a pathetic-looking dog was tied to a metal pole stuck into the ground. He licked his lips and yawned contentedly in the midst of his littered surroundings.

"Some watchdog," Jerry said. "I hope they're giving that poor thing some water."

Suzanne noticed that the house was similar to the one they were there to look at. It was the same shape, size and style. There were a few slight variations, but it even had the same kind of aluminum siding, except it was pale yellow.

Positioned to the right side of the house was another ramshackle-looking residence. Although it was much smaller, it was apparent that it had been built by the same builder, as the structural design resembled that of the other two houses. It was in dreadful shape, with the exception of a new roof.

On the front porch were some mismatched kitchen chairs and a green lounging chair, the outdoor kind that has plastic-covered cushions. It had been mended with duct tape and looked as if it would collapse if anyone sat on it. The screen door was swinging on its hinges as the wind blew it back and forth. There was one lone tree in the front yard, and it was huge. It provided a canopy over the entire yard.

Suzanne looked at Jerry for a reaction, but he didn't have a visible appearance of concern. He was looking at the house with slight interest, nothing more.

Suzanne retrieved the key to the front door from the side of the house where the realtor had told her to find it. She unlocked the door, and they stepped inside. The front room was a big square room with a couple of long, narrow windows along the left wall. There were new looking, though ill-fitting blinds on the windows. It looked and smelled as if the place had been recently painted.

Right away Jerry and Suzanne noticed the large baseboards and substantial-looking moldings used in the rooms. It seemed that this house had once belonged to someone of means. There were fancy doorknobs on the French doors that separated the front entry from the room on the right.

Throughout the house, there were wooden floors, but they were low-quality, yardstick-sized slats that had declined with age. In some areas, the brittle flooring was missing, most likely because of wear and tear, and the sub floor underneath was visible.

"These floors will be the first to go. Look at this cheap stuff." Jerry slid his foot under one of the loose boards, easily lifting it.

One of the jobs he had done in the past dealt with hardwood flooring, so he could easily envision what new oak floors could do for a place like this. He walked around the room testing for soft spots in the floor. In various places, he noticed that it felt spongy. He also listened for creaks as he walked, stepping back and forth in areas that made noise.

As Jerry studied the floors closer, he noticed that there was a prominent lean toward the right side of the house. It was evident that a lot of work would need to be done to get the house leveled before new flooring could be installed.

Straight ahead, in what was most likely meant to be a dining room, there was a lovely fireplace. The hearth was antique marble and a beautiful tiger oak mantel was mounted to the wall. Jerry paused and admired the grain of the wood before resuming his tour of the house.

The kitchen was the next room they entered. The original cabinets had been torn out at some point, and there were some new, unfinished ones sitting in the middle of the floor. There were no handles on the cabinet doors, which were generic-looking with no finishing details.

The kitchen was small, and it had a pantry toward the back of the room about the size of a closet with crude shelves built against the wall. Adjacent to the pantry was a screened-in back porch that looked like it was an afterthought when it was built onto the house. There were piles of newspapers, pieces of wood, and other trash stacked around in it.

"I wouldn't stand out there too long. That porch might just fall right out from under you," Jerry warned Suzanne.

"Yeah, and I'm sure there are a million spiders out here, too!" Suzanne cringed as she quickly, but tentatively, stepped back into the house.

The next room off the kitchen was in keeping with the rest of the house. It was a big square room with high ceilings. "I guess this must be a bedroom," Jerry said as he tested the closet door. "This was added sometime later. Houses built back then didn't have closets."

There was a large floor-to-ceiling window along the back wall that generously allowed a stream of sunlight into the room. Jerry noticed that the window had been painted shut. "You'd play hell trying to get that thing open."

In the next room they came to, there was a broken toilet and rust-stained claw foot tub sitting unattached in the middle of the floor. This was also probably meant to be a bedroom, but was obviously being used as storage for the plumbing fixtures from the bathroom.

"Gross!" Suzanne said as she looked at the commode and tub. "That toilet has got to go, but you know, the tub has some possibilities."

Jerry bent down and examined it. "There are probably a dozen coats of paint on it, but a person could put some work into that old thing and it could be really cool looking. I always liked claw foot tubs."

Suzanne teased, "If I didn't know better, I'd think you might like this place."

"Oh, I don't know. Maybe," Jerry said in his most non-committal tone of voice.

The next area they explored was what had been the only bathroom in the house. The reason the plumbing was no longer hooked up was due to the floor being replaced, as evidenced by raw plywood.

Finally, there was one more room on the first floor that was undoubtedly used as a living room or parlor due to the proximity of it toward the front of the house. It was the large room with French doors located to the right as they had first entered the house. This completed the circle of rooms throughout the first floor.

The steps that led to the second floor were rough-sawn boards that had been painted white. The upstairs area had originally been an attic and had been turned into a crude living area consisting of two big, mostly unfinished rooms. The low-hung ceilings were barely tall enough to accommodate the windows.

Suzanne was amused to see Jerry duck his head as if the ceiling was too low for him to stand upright. "The ceiling is not that low, for heaven's sake!"

"Yeah, but I'm extremely tall," Jerry said with a serious look on his face.

Suzanne smiled at him and shook her head as she walked around looking at the details of the rooms. At some point, someone had worked on this area just enough so that someone could use it for sleeping. There was an old mattress laying on the floor and other evidence of use, even though there wasn't any heating or air conditioning in that part of the house.

"This is where you'll sleep," Jerry said with a smirk.

"Uh, I don't think so. You can sleep up here with the ghosts."

"Oh, come on now, no self-respecting ghost would live up here."

Heading back downstairs, they decided to take a look at the basement. It was a damp-smelling area with dirt walls that came almost to the steps. Trash was heaped everywhere including shredded newspapers that had been fashioned into rats' nests.

"Yuck. Let's go upstairs. I get the willies just being down here," Suzanne said as she turned to go back to the main floor.

"You know, this really has been a fine house in its day," Jerry said mostly to himself as they walked around the rooms of the house for a second time. "The trim around the doors and windows is really nice looking. See how thick it is?" He ran his hand along the wood around one of the doorways.

"Yeah, it has been a nice place in time, but it needs a lot of work."

"The floors bother me being so uneven." Jerry pointed toward the front room to the right of the entry. "It'll probably need foundation work or some extra supports to make it level."

"Jerry, do you think we can do this? I mean, we could get the foundation worked on and put in some new floors. The kitchen will need to have the cabinets painted and mounted."

"I don't know…"

Suzanne sighed and looked at the French doors. "Sure, it would be hard work, but this would be a beautiful place when we get done with it."

Jerry studied the fireplace and walked around a while longer. He and Suzanne had already made plans to split up, but he wasn't sure if he was ready for their marriage to end. And now, Suzanne seemed eager to get back together to work on a project with him. He wasn't sure how to respond to her.

Jerry's plan had been to move to Florida to be with his parents, but if this house deal became a reality, he was willing to stay. He and Suzanne had done small remodeling jobs together before, and he knew they worked well as a team. The thought of saving their relationship was worth the effort. Maybe this house was just what they needed to bring them back together again.

"Well, yeah, it would be a nice place when we get done with it," Jerry said as he observed an old fashioned push-button light switch. He leaned against the doorway thinking.

"What do you think? Would you be willing to go in on this with me?" Suzanne asked.

"I guess so. I don't know. This would take some time, getting all of this done. I like the house. I guess I'd be willing to try it," Jerry answered, cautiously pausing between statements.

"Are you serious?" Suzanne asked with a smile. "Don't be pulling my leg."

"Yeah, I'm serious. I mean, I guess I am…"

She waited for Jerry to say something else, but he just smiled back at her. "Okay, I'll call and make an offer!" Suzanne jumped up and down clapping her hands. Jerry watched her dance around with excitement and thought about how much he wanted things to work out between them.

Suzanne looked young for her twenty-seven years. She was a petite woman, which would make it seem as though she would be unable to take on such a huge physical project. But he knew that when she was faced with a challenge, she was a force to be reckoned with. Jerry felt optimistic as he playfully ushered her to the door.

"Well, Madame Homebuyer, let's get out of here and grab some lunch," Jerry said as they walked out of the house. Closing the door behind him, he looked back through the window of the front door at the fireplace staring back at him. This could definitely be a nice place to live.

Chapter 3

Jerry and Suzanne headed down the concrete walkway toward the truck parked on the street. As they got to the sidewalk, they looked up to see someone walking toward them. It was a lady with a cane, although she seemed to manage fine without the use of it. At first glance, she looked to be in her fifties. She was overweight, wearing gaudy, out of date clothing. A straw hat sat crooked on her head.

"Hi," she said as she walked closer. She didn't say it as much as she called it out in a singsong, whiney voice. Her eyes weren't focused on any one thing, just glancing around nonchalantly as if she was in a world all her own.

She stopped when she got close enough to have a conversation and looked at Jerry and Suzanne with a grin. "Hi," she said again.

Jerry nodded to her and replied, "Hey, there. Pretty day, huh?"

She was slow to respond, her eyes finally settling on Jerry's face. She answered, "Yeahhh . . ." her voice trailing off as if she was thinking about something else.

"My name is Jerry, and this is my wife Suzanne," Jerry said as he extended his hand to her. "We're thinking about buying this old house."

The lady's smile broadened as she shook his hand. "My name is Gladys. I live right there." She pointed her cane toward the run-down house next door. "My husband passed away last year. He paid off my house before he died."

"Oh, well, that's good." Suzanne didn't know what else to say.

Gladys answered, "Yeahhh . . ."

There was a long pause. "We'll be back soon. You'll probably be seeing a lot of us in the future," Jerry said cheerfully as he stepped off the curb and into Suzanne's truck.

As they pulled away from the curb, Suzanne said, "I think something's wrong with that lady."

"It looks like she has some kind of mental problem or something. She was nice enough, though," Jerry answered.

"I guess so. It's kind of sad."

Suzanne paid close attention to the rest of the neighborhood as she drove away from the house. The streets were lined with million-dollar homes intermingled with small, shotgun rental houses. Although it was officially designated as an historic neighborhood, it was far from the picturesque vision of lovely turn-of-the-century houses with magnolia trees and crepe myrtles that comes to mind. It was the haves living next to the have-nots.

Most of the historic houses had been built in the late 1800's and early 1900's. There were Queen Anne's, Bungalows, Cottages, and Craftsman-style homes. Some were in excellent shape, while others seemed to be in a perpetual state of rehabilitation. Still, others hadn't been touched in years, looking as if they needed to be demolished altogether. It was a shame that so many years had gone by and no one had taken the time to preserve more of these historic structures.

The next couple of days went by quickly. Suzanne called the realtor, Bruce Stuart, who had the house listed and made an appointment to meet with him to sign the paperwork. They met at Bruce's house, which also served as his office, to sign the contract.

Bruce's house was a beautiful, old historic home with a broad front porch and double front doors. Bruce met Jerry and

Suzanne at the door along with two willowy-looking dogs at his side. Suzanne noticed that Bruce was quite feminine and looked at Jerry with raised eyebrows to see if he noticed, too. He looked back with a knowing smile, which made Suzanne want to laugh. They followed him through his extravagant rooms to his office.

When Jerry and Suzanne sat down, Bruce offered them coffee, which they politely declined, so he sat behind his desk and proceeded to start writing out the contract longhand.

"The owner is a good friend of mine," Bruce said. "As a matter of fact, my dogs are her dog's brother and sister." He continued to write the details of the contract, his boney fingers tapping on the table as he thought between details he was writing. "I would have bought that house myself, but we're just too good of friends and I couldn't do that." He didn't look up from his papers as he talked.

Jerry and Suzanne weren't really sure what he meant, but being absorbed in the moment, they weren't interested in dissecting the conversation. They looked around the room as Bruce finished his writing. His office was beautiful with a cherry desk and bookcases, and best of all; he had a huge window that looked out onto the vast front porch. The room was bathed in light and felt warm and safe.

Bruce came around his desk and knelt on one knee to describe the details of the contract. He explained that it was an owner-terms agreement. When he got to the point of explaining the section of the contract regarding the termite inspection, he said, "I know there's some termite damage, but the owner won't be willing to fix it. You're getting such a good deal on this house; I'm just going to cross out the part about a termite inspection." There was some information he had written down and then crossed out. He talked so quickly and with such authority that Jerry and Suzanne just nodded in agreement. Toward the end of the contract, Bruce explained the last clause he had written in the document, stating that if the house was sold within five years, there would be a $10,000 pre-payment penalty.

"Now if you two decide to divorce in the next couple of years and you have to sell the house, you'll have that pre-payment penalty to deal with," Bruce said in a tone that Suzanne couldn't identify. Was this a forewarning of some kind? It felt like an omen, but Suzanne rationalized her apprehensive thoughts as nervousness.

Jerry looked at Suzanne to get her reaction. She could tell he was looking at her, but she kept her eyes on the realtor as he spoke, afraid to give any indication that his comment about splitting up had any impact on her. She knew they both wanted to make this deal happen and ultimately make their marriage work.

"No, if we put a bunch of work and money into a place, we intend to stay there forever, right?" Suzanne said to Jerry.

"Oh yeah, definitely," Jerry replied.

They reluctantly agreed that the pre-payment penalty was okay, paid their earnest money, and left. The final closing of the house was set for the following week.

The more Jerry thought about the pre-payment penalty, the more he realized he didn't like the sound of it. "That's a lot of money. Maybe the homeowner could drop some of that for us. I think it's just too much."

Suzanne answered, "Well, like we discussed, if we put all that work into the house, I'm not leaving there for a long time. Remember, we talked about this already. I really don't think it's an issue. Besides, we're going to have so much money tied up in the place; it'll take that long before we could get our investment out of it if we decide to sell it."

Suzanne sounded so convincing that Jerry grudgingly agreed with her. Somehow he felt like this issue would come back to bite him later, but in trying to keep the peace and move forward, he agreed that it would be alright.

Chapter 4

After leaving the meeting with the realtor, Suzanne went back to work. Moments after returning to her desk, she got the message that her mother had taken a turn for the worse. She immediately called Jerry after getting off the phone with the nurse.

"Jerry, we need to get to the hospital to see Mama. I just spoke to her nurse, and she's not doing too well."

After stopping by Jerry's house to pick him up, Suzanne rushed to the hospital, paying little attention to the speed limit signs. "Jerry, this really sounds bad. When I spoke to the nurse this morning, she told me that Mama may have to go onto a respirator."

Jerry opened the window a little to let in some air. "What do you think your mother would say about us buying a house together?"

"Oh, I don't know. I'm sure she would be happy for us," Suzanne answered. She knew Ruth would not be pleased; in fact, she would likely disapprove. Suzanne didn't feel like talking about the house, and she sure didn't want to go into any conversation with Jerry about how her mother would feel about it. Suzanne felt anxious as she pulled into the hospital parking lot and looked for a parking spot close to the entrance.

Suzanne decided she wouldn't say anything about buying the house to her mother. It wasn't important right now anyway. Suzanne closed her eyes and whispered, "Please, Lord, don't let anything happen to Mama."

Once they got to the intensive care unit, they waited several minutes for the visiting hour to begin, during which time a nurse asked them to put on gowns, gloves and face masks before they entered Ruth's room. It was still undetermined what was wrong with Ruth, and the hospital was taking no chances of spreading disease. It seemed a little late for that, Suzanne thought, since just two days ago she kissed her mother goodbye when she left the hospital.

When Suzanne stepped into Ruth's room, she saw that her mother's condition had gotten worse. Suzanne pulled up a chair next to her mother and reached out to hold her hand. "How are you feeling today?" Suzanne asked. She smiled and tried not to look overly concerned.

"I'm alright, I guess. These nurses are so hateful, though. Sick as I am, that fat one smarts off to me every time she comes in here," Ruth said. She pulled back the sheet and fanned it. "It's so hot in here. I can hardly catch my breath." Ruth was wheezing as she struggled to breathe. She had oxygen tubes in her nose and IV needles in her arms. Her eyes looked weary and her lips were cracked and dry. "Can you get me some more water?" she said as she nodded toward her cup sitting on the table.

As Suzanne stood to reach for the cup, Jerry said to Ruth, "Put out your hand." Ruth looked at him for a few seconds.

Suzanne cringed. She turned her back to both Ruth and Jerry to rinse the cup in the sink. She was glad they couldn't see the expression on her face. Why is he doing this now? Suzanne thought. This is not the time.

"Okay," Ruth said as she did what he asked. Jerry placed the key in the palm of her hand. Ruth looked at it and asked, "What's this?"

"It's the key to the house that Suzanne and I are buying," Jerry said, smiling. He waited for Ruth's reaction, which was slow in coming.

"You're buying a house?" she asked.   She looked disappointed, but remained polite.   Her hand was trembling as she handed the key back to Jerry.   "Where is it?"

Suzanne managed a smile as she came back with a fresh cup of water and held it while her mother took a drink from the straw.   Ruth closed her eyes as she drank.   She looked so exhausted; Suzanne wondered if she was going to fall asleep every time she closed her eyes.

Shooting an aggravated look toward Jerry, Suzanne intercepted the question.   "Well, Mama, it's close to downtown, and it's an older house that needs some work, but it's really going to be nice when we get done with it."   Suzanne could feel her mother studying her.   It was becoming an awkward moment.   The last thing she wanted to do was upset her mother, and she wished that the subject had never been brought up.

"Hmmm.   Congratulations, I guess," said Ruth.   She didn't try to mask her displeasure as she changed the subject.   She looked up at the television.   "I'm so sick of this stupid crap they have on TV these days.   None of it makes a bit of sense."   Ruth's voice was weak as she laid her head back on her pillow.

Jerry went down the hall to get some coffee while Suzanne sat next to her mother's bed.   After he walked out of the room, Ruth asked, "Haven't you signed those papers yet?"   She frowned at Suzanne.   She was referring to the divorce papers that Suzanne had been holding onto since she had filed for divorce over six months ago.

"Well, no, we decided to buy this house together and we'll see how it goes," Suzanne answered, trying to placate her mother.   She felt silly having a serious discussion while wearing a mask on her face.   She could see it move up and down as she talked.

"You know things ain't going to change.   You'll be working all the time, and carrying the weight of everything on them little shoulders." Ruth had a pleading look in her eyes as she spoke. "I don't think it's a good idea at all."

"It'll be alright, Mama. You know Jerry's a good guy and I think we can get along enough to get this house done." Suzanne tried to soothe her mother, but when she realized Ruth's mind was made up about Jerry, her defensive nature stepped in. "I know what I'm doing." She smiled at her mother warmly and put her arms around her. "Really, everything's going to be okay."

When Jerry got back into the room with his coffee, the direction of the conversation turned to Ruth's health. "What's the next step? Are they going to keep you in ICU?" Jerry asked as he raised his mask to sip his coffee. Suzanne was amazed that a nurse didn't waylay him as he came back into the room with it.

"I guess they're going to take some more x-rays of my lungs tomorrow. I don't really know." Ruth was struggling to breathe. She looked up at the television again.

"We'll talk to your nurse before we leave to see what's going on," said Suzanne. "Our time is up, but we'll be back to see you tomorrow. If you think of anything you need, call me or Daddy."

"I need some slippers. When I get up to start walking again, I'm going to need some slippers," Ruth said.

"Okay, I'll get you some," Suzanne replied as she gave her mother a hug goodbye. "I'll see you tomorrow."

After they left the room, Suzanne asked her mother's nurse who was standing in the hall, "When is her doctor going to be here again? I need to talk to him." Suzanne felt her face flush and wanted to sit down somewhere. "Does he even know what's wrong with her yet?"

The nurse looked at Suzanne sympathetically. "Her doctor will be here tomorrow morning if you want to talk to him. He's really the one to tell you what your mom can expect next.

Or I can have him paged if you feel like you need to talk to him today."

"No, that's okay, I'll talk to him tomorrow," she said. After thanking the nurse, Suzanne turned to Jerry. "I really need to get out of here. Let's go get something to eat." Suzanne felt drained. She didn't even have the strength to confront him about bringing up the house in front of Ruth.

"Sounds good to me," Jerry answered softly and held Suzanne's hand. "Hey, try not to worry. Your mama's going to be okay," he said as he pushed the elevator button. "She'll get through this and she'll come home."

"Jerry, what if she dies?" Suzanne could feel tears stinging her eyes.

"Listen, whatever happens, I'll be right here beside you and we'll get through this together," Jerry said as he put his arm around Suzanne's shoulders. "They still don't even know what's wrong with her. Maybe they'll figure it out and she'll get better."

Suzanne knew in her heart what Jerry was saying wasn't true. She knew that she'd soon have to deal with her mother's death, a funeral, and the future without her mother's support. She felt hopeless and lonely just thinking about it.

Chapter 5

R uth was placed on life support a couple of days later. At first, she went in and out of consciousness as the respirator forced air into her weak lungs. After a few days, she slipped into a semi-comatose state, occasionally indicating that she recognized someone's voice by blinking her eyes or moving her fingers. Ruth was dying. Everyone in the family finally had to admit it was inevitable.

After a week of trying different therapies that ultimately didn't work, the doctor advised the family that Ruth's vital organs were beginning to shut down and could no longer function enough to keep her alive. He showed little emotion as he informed the dying woman's family that there was no hope.

Everyone looked at each other in silence for a few minutes. The small family counseling room was bright with fluorescent light, and it cast a sickly pallor to their somber faces. The family concluded that the next morning Ruth would be taken off life support. The doctor nodded in agreement and turned to leave the room.

As the doctor walked out the door, Suzanne's father, Paul, touched his arm and asked, "Is there any chance she could survive? Shouldn't we give it more time?" His voice was desperate. The doctor didn't answer, but he patted Paul's shoulder. It was the closest thing to compassion that Suzanne had seen out of this doctor, and it seemed forced.

The next few days went by quickly as funeral arrangements were made, and the family learned how to deal with grief.

Ruth didn't have a decent dress to be buried in, so Elaine, Suzanne, and Jerry went to buy one for her. They picked a beautiful, dark blue dress made of a silky material. Suzanne looked at the price tag. "This thing is eighty dollars! Mama would never buy something this expensive." Suzanne suddenly felt a deep sorrow that overwhelmed her. Ruth was too young to die at age fifty-nine.

Suzanne and Elaine decided to buy the dress. "You know they'll cut it right up the back, don't you?" Elaine asked.

"You mean to get it on her? I never thought about it," Suzanne answered, a little surprised at Elaine's comment. Suzanne was trying to concentrate on the funeral arrangements, but she kept imagining trying to get a dress on a corpse. The morbid thought made her sick to her stomach.

Elaine and Suzanne then went through the process of picking out a casket for their mother. It was an exhaustive ordeal made worse by the auto salesman-like air of the funeral home director who was selling the casket. He described the lead-lined coffin in great detail. His spiel seemed to go on forever. The one they finally agreed upon had a shiny blue finish with off-white satin material for the lining. It even had a pillow, which looked pretty comfortable. Suzanne thought about how it would feel to lay her head down on it.

Before the first visitors arrived at the funeral home to pay their respects to Ruth, the family had time to say their goodbyes in private. Suzanne walked up to the casket to look at her mother, barely noticing the holy cross pattern sewn into the fabric of the lid.

Suzanne first focused on Ruth's hands, folded on her chest. Automatically, Suzanne's memories of her mother refinishing furniture, something she often did for enjoyment and a little extra income, came to mind. Ruth had always complained about how much she hated the way her hands looked. She said they were manly looking. Suzanne had a lump in her throat as she remembered how tender her mother's hands could be.

Suzanne's eyes then worked their way up to her mother's face. Ruth looked like she did before she got sick. It was amazing what makeup could do. Suzanne felt strangely comforted, and she reached out to touch her mother's cheek. It felt like cold leather.

Suzanne spent the afternoon talking to family and friends that she hadn't seen in years. After the funeral service, several family members went to Paul's house to eat and visit with each other. Paul was going through the motions of reminiscing with relatives, but Suzanne saw loneliness and pain in his eyes. She could barely hold a normal conversation with anyone without glancing at him across the room. She was worried about him, but she knew that he'd eventually overcome his grief.

The next week, it was back to work and back to reality. Suzanne was grateful that she had a distraction like the house project to keep her busy and get her mind off the sadness of losing her mother. It promised to be a worthwhile diversion, and at the same time she hoped it would help do some healing between Jerry and her.

Since they hadn't been living together when they purchased the house, it was going to be a big adjustment for them to move back in together. Suzanne had grown distant during the separation. This was a feeling that had to change. Relying on Jerry through the death of her mother was one thing, but putting any remaining animosity aside would be a challenge. She had to grow up, and she had to find it within herself to put the past behind her. She hoped Jerry could do the same.

"Tell me again why you're going to do this crazy scheme with Jerry," Elaine asked Suzanne as they sat in the floor going through their mother's jewelry box. Elaine's eyes were wide with anticipation of an answer.

Suzanne wanted to laugh at Elaine's expression, but she remained serious. "You know, when Jerry and I got married, he was really the only person I'd ever known. I mean, in a romantic way. I mean, well, you know what I mean."

"Okay. And?"

"Well, I never dated anyone else seriously before getting married, and during the year that Jerry and I were separated, the guys I went out with turned out to be losers. What a waste of time that was." She studied an earring that she found in the jewelry box. "What's wrong with giving life with Jerry another chance?" She felt defensive of her decision and wished that she could change the subject.

"Suzanne, you're getting back together with him because he's a nice guy, not because you're in love with him. I know you care about him, but after all the problems you two have had, can that turn into a lifetime commitment?"

Suzanne paused before answering. Elaine was right, but Suzanne was too stubborn to admit it. "With no one to lean on while Mama was sick and dying, I was able to turn to him and he was so supportive and caring. Salvaging our marriage seems like the right thing to do. Besides, we've been married for nine years already."

"Those are not good enough reasons to go into this big house thing together. Why not ease back into a relationship? Do you have to move back in together right away?"

"Really, it's too late. We've already started this process. We can't stop now." Suzanne sighed and tried to put an end to the conversation as she stood up from sitting on the floor. "Please try to be happy for me. I'm so excited about this. Okay?"

"Okay, okay! Just don't make me say I told you so."

Jerry gave his notice to the owners of the duplex he'd been renting while he and Suzanne were separated; the same one they'd shared when they were together. He moved his belongings into a storage unit, and began staying with Suzanne in the apartment that she had rented when she moved out.

Jerry didn't have a full-time job and had relied on sporadic carpentry jobs to keep his bills paid. They decided that it made sense for Suzanne to continue her full-time job and work on the house in the evenings and on the weekends. Jerry's primary responsibility was going to be working on the house, at least until it was livable. Suzanne believed she could manage, using her paycheck and what little savings they had, to maintain monthly payments on both places for a couple of months until the house was ready to be moved into.

"We should probably be able to start living in the house before Christmas, don't you think?" Suzanne asked Jerry.

"Oh, yeah. We may not have it completely finished, but by Christmas we should be able to move in," Jerry answered.

The thought of Christmas without her mother deeply saddened her. She tried not to think about it, and instead fantasized about a big Christmas tree in their new house. She closed her eyes and could see it in her mind . . . a tall, beautifully decorated tree standing in the corner of the entryway, lights shining through the front windows for the neighbors to see. She imagined a roaring fire in the fireplace. She'd never had a home of her own, and the visions of contentment made her feel warm and joyful.

Chapter 6

The first weekend after the closing of 2010 Cumberland Street, Jerry and Suzanne headed to their newly-acquired house and started working on their new project. Jerry had rented a large trash receptacle from the city and stationed it in the back yard. Already, after only a day's work, it was halfway filled with a pile of trash from the back yard and some junk that was sitting around the house, including the commode.

Feeling eager about starting on the interior of the house, Suzanne began the task of removing the wooden flooring from the main floor of the house. She used a shovel-type tool which was actually designed to remove shingles from a roof, but it worked well. Suzanne was pleased that the boards came up easily as they were dry and quite brittle. They had been painted green at some point, and Suzanne was relieved to be getting rid of the evidence of the "bad taste" someone had to actually paint a wooden floor. With every few feet Suzanne uncovered of the sub floor, she was feeling more satisfied with her progress. Her excitement was matched with Jerry's as he took turns with her to tear out the old floorboards.

From outside, there was a humming noise.

"Stop for just a second," Suzanne said to Jerry.

Jerry stopped working so he could listen. It was singing, not very loud, but audible above the sounds of work in the house. Suzanne looked through the blinds toward the neighbor's house and saw Gladys sitting on her porch at the foot-end of her green, duct-taped chaise lounge. Her back was to Suzanne as she rocked back and forth humming. Most of the chair she was sitting on was taken up by her large rear-end, and a skinny yellow cat was lying next to her. Her steely gray hair was in ponytails all over her head, and she was smoking a cigarette. Since the houses were only a few feet apart, Suzanne could clearly see a pack of generic cigarettes on a small table next to Gladys along with an ash tray and lighter.

"It's just Gladys next door. Jerry, she looks sort of lonely out there all by herself. Do you think she's okay? She's moaning and rocking." Suzanne squinted through the blinds to watch her neighbor.

Jerry rolled his eyes and smiled. "I don't think she's moaning. I think she's singing, and she looks pretty darn happy to me most of the time."

Jerry and Suzanne continued with their work on the floor for a few more hours, and then decided to call it a day. They felt good about what had been accomplished, but they knew that before much more work could be done on the inside of the house, the foundation problems had to be addressed. The sagging floors and the extreme incline of the house needed to be repaired before any other big projects could be started. It was satisfying, however, to be doing something, anything, to their new house.

The routine began the next week. Suzanne went to work at the office during the day, stopped by the apartment to change clothes, and then joined Jerry to work on the house late into the night, only to get up and do it all over again the next day. The enthusiasm of a new project kept them motivated, even when they were so exhausted all they wanted to do was fall into bed for a few hours of sleep.

Jerry and Suzanne already knew there'd been a termite problem in the house. It had been treated for termites since they'd acquired it to prevent further damage from occurring.

They also knew that the termites had done some destruction that affected the foundation of the house. Jerry obtained estimates from a couple of foundation professionals. One promised to repair the problem within a couple of weeks, but he was too expensive. The contractor Jerry settled on was a man named Robbie Perry. He had worked on historic homes in the neighborhood, and he seemed to be the best choice to work on their house. He prided himself on being a purist in regards to keeping historic homes true to their original construction.

Robbie commended Jerry for not going with the foundation repair company that promised to lift the house quickly. He told Jerry that such a rushed, drastic change in the house's foundation could damage the rest of the house to the degree that there would be irreparable harm done to the structure of it.

The construction of the foundation, like some other homes in older neighborhoods, consisted of rough pine posts on which the house rested. Beneath the pine posts were flat rocks used as footers. No concrete was used in the foundation. As a result, over time, the posts had settled into the ground, somewhat rotting away, giving the house a considerable pitch toward the back that had to be lifted in order to make the house level.

The termite damage hadn't affected the foundation posts as much as it had weakened the support beams and flooring joists of the house. The floor joists and the main load-bearing beams had been destroyed to the point that they gave way when they were hit with any force whatsoever. Therefore, the first major project was to lift the house, replace the main supports and some of the joists, and put new, pressure-treated six-by-six posts in place of the old pine posts that had held the house up for the previous eighty-three years.

Since the house had to be lifted anyway, Jerry and Suzanne decided that they would go ahead and dig out the foundation area of the house to make a basement. This would require additional work and more money than they originally planned on spending, but Jerry felt that it would increase the value of the house and make the rehabilitation easier in the long run.

Jerry hired the son of one of their previous neighbors to help with the renovation. Gilbert Carver was seventeen-years-old, and he seemed to be a polite, trustworthy young man. He was offered the same pay per hour as he was making working at the local grocery store, and he gladly accepted.

Gilbert began showing up at the house after school and on weekends to work on the house. Sometimes he brought his friend Carl to help, but mostly he just came by himself. It turned out Gilbert was reliable and hard working, and he was a lot of fun to have around.

Suzanne called Jerry from work to find out how he was doing with the house. The contractor was there, and Jerry was helping him get set up in the basement.

"Well, I can see we already have a problem," Jerry told Suzanne.

"What's that?"

"Gladys next door," Jerry answered flatly.

"What happened?"

"She came over here today asking for five dollars. I told her I was sorry, but I don't have any money. If she ever asks you, don't ever give her any. We don't want to get started with that," Jerry answered.

"Well, she already asks us to do favors for her. She's going to have to realize that even though we can help her sometimes, we're not there for her to use anytime she wants. You were definitely right to say no. Besides, we're broke. We don't have any money to be giving to her."

"We didn't take her on to raise along with everything else we have to do," Jerry said. "Well, I guess I better get back to it. See you when you get home."

Jerry removed an eight-foot wide portion of the siding in the back of the house where the foundation met the ground so that dirt could be hauled out of the basement by wheelbarrow and shoring up of the house could begin. For several hours every day, Suzanne, Jerry, Gilbert, and Carl filled the wheelbarrow with dirt and dumped the contents into a big pile toward the back of the lot. Everyone took turns pushing the dirt-filled wheelbarrow, except Suzanne, who was assigned as a permanent digger.

As they dug out the basement dirt, they found empty bottles, trash, and old newspapers from the 1930's and 1940's. This went on for a couple of weeks, until a four-foot walkway slowly emerged from the middle of the basement through the back of the house. There were at least five hundred wheelbarrows of dirt pushed up and out of the basement over the next couple of weeks.

As work progressed on the house, it was evident that the contractor, who had been hired to help with the leveling of the house, wasn't dependable. If Robbie said he'd be at the house at nine o'clock, he would show up at eleven o'clock, if at all. Occasionally, he'd call and say that he couldn't make it, and sometimes Jerry didn't hear from him for a day or two.

When Robbie did show up at the house, the quality of his work was undeniably first-rate. He brought his hydraulic house-jacks, and along with the steel beam Jerry had purchased at a salvage yard, he proceeded to prepare the house to be lifted. As he set up each jack he was keenly aware of what had to be accomplished, and he deliberately placed each one in its most effective place at the foundation of the house.

Jerry and Robbie began lifting the back of the house to the appropriate level. It was a slow process that would take several weeks to complete. As the house was lifted, the whole structure was affected including the roof, the porch, and the drywall inside the house. Jerry tried not to think about the residual work that would have to be done to fix stress-related cracks in the walls. He was grateful that the plaster walls had been replaced with drywall. Fixing crumbling plaster throughout the house would've been a disaster. He hoped the windows wouldn't break under the pressure; it would be expensive to replace them.

One evening while Suzanne, Jerry, and Gilbert were digging dirt in the basement, Suzanne looked up between the ground and the elevated bottom of the house to see a pair of boots above her head. Frank, Gladys' son from next door, leaned down and said, "Somebody parked in front of our house. My mother told me to come over here and tell y'all to move your truck."

"Oh, I'm sorry. I'll tell Gilbert to get out there and move it," Suzanne said. She asked Gilbert to go ahead and park somewhere else. Even though it was a public street, and there were no laws against parking in front of a neighbor's house, Suzanne wanted to keep the peace and wasn't looking to make the neighbors angry.

Gilbert went to move his truck, and when he came back, he was unusually quiet. He worked on picking up tools and getting ready to leave, saying that he had to be home early.

"Are you okay?" Jerry asked.

"Yeah, I'm fine," Gilbert said as he wrapped an extension cord that wasn't being used.

Suzanne was folding big sheets of plastic. "Are you sure?" She could tell he was trying to avoid their questions.

Gilbert unhooked his jacket from a nail on a post and started putting it on. He pulled his keys out of his pocket and looked at them as he spoke. "That guy next door, the one who said for me to move my truck, said something smart to me."

"What did he say?" asked Suzanne. She didn't like the feeling she was getting about this. Jerry stopped working to listen.

"Aw, it really wasn't anything. He just said I better watch it," Gilbert answered trying to blow it off.

"He said you better watch it? Is that all he said?" Jerry asked.

"Well, pretty much. He just said don't park in front of my house again. I said, okay, don't worry about it. Then he said, don't make me tell you again." Gilbert laughed to lighten the mood. "Really, it ain't no big deal. Hey, Jerry, what time do you want me to get over here tomorrow?"

"Nine o'clock would be okay. Hopefully, it'll stop raining, so we might be able to get some work done without sloshing around in puddles of water down here," Jerry answered.

After Gilbert left, Suzanne looked at Jerry. He was measuring a post. "I don't like what Frank said to Gilbert. Jerry, I'm afraid he's not going to want to come over and help us anymore. Why would Frank tell him to watch it? What if Frank tries something?"

"Ah, I'm not too worried about it. Frank's probably drunk or high. Besides, he's a puny thing. Gilbert can take care of himself," Jerry said.

Suzanne thought about the confrontation between Frank and Gilbert all evening. She woke from a deep sleep listening. She didn't know what she was listening for, but she was sure she felt something troubling in the air.

Chapter 7

G ilbert returned to work the next day, which was Saturday. He and Jerry got busy hauling more dirt with the wheelbarrow. To get it out of the basement and into the back yard, Jerry had to cut back more of the wooden siding, which left a large portion of the basement area wide open.

It happened to be the year of El Nino, which brought torrential rains to the area. As a result, water streamed into the opening at the back of the house and partially flooded the basement. Water pooled in the areas where hydraulic jacks were placed and caused them to sink into the unstable ground, undoing what little progress that had been made. Since the house could only be raised an inch or so at a time, the process was a frustrating, time consuming ordeal.

In between rainstorms, Jerry hired a man with a bobcat to dig out the remaining dirt from the basement. He dug out half of the basement on his first appointment. An issue to be dealt with was what to do with the dirt itself. It had to be put somewhere when the bobcat removed it from the basement.

A couple of neighbors had uneven yards and welcomed the loads of dirt to be placed in low lying areas. The bobcat operator leveled out the dirt as much as possible as he dumped it on the neighbors' yards. Jerry then raked it flat, sowed grass seed, and covered the areas with straw to help the grass get a head start. This made for some happy neighbors, and it gave Jerry a place to put load after load of dirt.

Once the basement area had been cleared, Jerry and Robbie began preparing to shore up one entire side of the house with new support posts. Each six-by-six pressure-treated post would be set on twelve inches of reinforced concrete used as a footer. The digging of the footers was an enormous job in itself. Each footer hole had to be dug to a certain depth for stability. First, a post-hole digger was used to achieve depth. When they got to the point where they were deep enough into the ground, they used a hand-held tool to scrape out the remaining loose dirt and poured the concrete in the hole. A stick was inserted into the wet concrete and tapped lightly to remove air bubbles. The top surface was then smoothed out with the flat edge of a trowel and checked with a leveling tool to make sure it was perfectly flat and level.

In order to keep the basement as dry as possible, Jerry constructed a makeshift cover for the open area out of plastic sheeting. He anchored the plastic to the top of the opening and draped it out past the area where water could find its way under the house. The plastic could be pushed aside as needed when work was being done in the basement. It seemed like a good temporary solution.

The next Saturday morning, since electricity was needed for the rooms on the first floor, Jerry and Suzanne decided to take a break from working on the basement and concentrate their efforts on the electrical wiring for a change. The existing electrical system consisted of an antiquated fuse box and knob-and-tube wiring. Some of the insulation on the wiring had become frayed over the years, and it was no longer safe to use. As they were working, the house suddenly became dark. Jerry looked out the window at the black storm clouds gathering. Another thunderstorm was coming. More rain, more problems.

Jerry rushed out the back door and ran to the area behind the house where they had been walking in and out of the basement earlier that day. He pulled the plastic down around the opening at the back of the house and tried to straighten it as he dragged the end of it to the point where he thought the rain couldn't get under it.

Suzanne was right behind him throwing on a jacket as she ran into the backyard to help. They attempted to secure the plastic on the ground by placing large rocks or bricks on it to keep it from blowing out of control.

The wind had picked up, and leaves and debris were flying everywhere. Jerry was trying to catch the plastic as it blew out of his hands. It flew just out of his reach right as the rain and hail began to fall with intensity, thumping against his shoulders. The wind blew his hat off, which he tried to catch before it hit the ground. A gust of wind snatched it out of his grasp just as it landed. The icy hail pelted against Jerry's face as he struggled to get control of the plastic. The lightning scared Suzanne, but she wasn't about to leave Jerry to fight this storm alone.

Thunder boomed overhead as Jerry hollered to Suzanne to get in the house. Suzanne shook her head and refused to go inside as she grappled with the plastic, securing it as fast as she could with whatever heavy things she could find to put along the edges. She scooted a tire that was sitting in the yard onto one corner of it.

Jerry couldn't let the basement get flooded again. It was just too hard to get those supports right in the first place. "God, I don't expect you to help us, but damn it, don't do this to us!" Jerry was screaming at the sky. He looked like he was crying. Finally, he got control of the plastic and held it down with his foot, while Suzanne placed a concrete block on the final unrestrained corner to hold it to the ground.

They ran back into the house drenched head to toe. Standing at the back door watching the plastic to see if it stayed in place, Jerry said, "I guess that'll hold for a while. We just need to keep an eye on it to make sure the wind doesn't blow more rain into the basement." He was out of breath as he spoke. "We've got to keep that dry down there until we can get those posts in," Jerry said as he dried off with a t-shirt that was draped across a ladder just inside the door. Suzanne found a towel inside the house and began drying herself off. As she wiped her face, she turned her back to Jerry and cried quietly into the towel.

The rain didn't stop for several days and high winds accompanied the storms. The plastic kept blowing out of the way and the water got into the basement no matter how many times Jerry tried to hold it down with cement blocks or bricks. The wind was just too clever, and always found a weak spot to get underneath and blow the plastic into the air, revealing another spot for the water to leak into the basement.

As soon as the rain let up, Jerry got creative and built a wooden awning "skeleton" for the plastic sheeting to be fastened to so it wouldn't blow away. He used a staple gun and heavy-duty staples to secure the plastic to the wooden frame. This actually worked out well, and the basement stayed dry for the next several months.

Besides the constant threat of rainwater leaking into the basement, there were other problems working against the setting of the concrete. First of all, it was cold, and there was only plastic to shield the inside of the basement from the bitter December weather. During particularly cold snaps, the concrete took extra days to dry.

Then there was the matter of the humidity in the basement due to all the rain. Even when they were able to keep the area dry, there was a heavy humidity in the air that kept the concrete from drying as quickly as it should. It was disheartening when the hard work of an entire evening, digging and pouring concrete in footer holes, was in danger of being destroyed by the elements. Jerry and Suzanne listened to weather reports religiously. They didn't have a television set up yet, so the radio had become indispensable.

A steel beam that was used to level the center of the house front-to-back supported the entire length of the house. It was braced by the hydraulic jacks and had to be stabilized for the duration of the time it took to replace the foundation supports. Robbie pounded the dirt and packed it as well as he could underneath the jacks so they wouldn't falter. Even so, Jerry had to check the levelness of the house every morning as the jacks slowly sunk a little every day.

To replace each foundation post, that particular area of the house was temporarily raised by six-by-six posts poised between the hydraulic jack and the support band of the house. Robbie raised each post slowly and listened to the house "pop" with each pump of the hydraulic jack. He shushed anyone who dared to talk during this procedure. The look on his face was intense as he listened to the house moan and groan with resistance. Because there were thousands of pounds of pressure on each post, everyone was warned to step back in case the post popped out of place and went flying.

Once an area of the house was lifted to the appropriate height for the new post, it was cut according to precise measurements. It was then hammered in its place on top of the new concrete footer that had been poured a couple of nights before. This was done as gently as possible so that the footer didn't crumble. After the post was found to be level, the jack holding the temporary post was slowly lowered to allow the weight of the house to sit on its new support. This was an extremely long and drawn-out process, as there were eight supports along one wall, five along two other walls, and five that spanned the new center main support beams for the house.

The cold winter air poured into the basement area where Jerry and Suzanne worked. They dressed in several shirts and jackets, peeling them off one by one as they exerted themselves digging footer holes. Most days they worked far into the evening, their hands numb from the cold, their muscles sore from digging. Suzanne fell into bed late each night and got up to go to work again the next day after only a few hours of sleep. Jerry's days consisted of more of the same, the never ending foundation project.

Eating was something that they only took a break to do because they had to keep up their energy. When Suzanne looked in the mirror, she noticed her lips were chapped from working in the cold basement all night. We've got to start taking better care of ourselves, Suzanne thought as she went to bed one night, still dressed in dirty work clothes.

This exhausting schedule went on for weeks. They knew, however, that the rest of the rehabilitation of the house was on hold until the basement was totally level and complete. Therefore, they endured what they considered to be short-lived inconveniences.

Robbie Perry had become completely undependable and had begun missing work with no explanation. Jerry worked by himself all day and Suzanne joined him after work to dig the last of the footers. At least Jerry had learned enough about the process before Robbie bailed out on him to finish in his absence.

After the posts were in position and completely leveled, the walls of the basement were installed. Jerry used thick plastic to shield the pressure-treated plywood basement walls from the dirt of the ground. The walls were screwed and nailed into place against the new support posts. As each piece of plywood was put into place, the amount of cold air coming into the basement was reduced making the area more comfortable to work in.

With the installation of each wall of plywood, Gilbert stapled insulation over it and a second piece of plywood sandwiched the insulation in place. The pressure-treated plywood had also been rolled with paint that had been treated with an insect-repellant additive as an extra measure of protection.

It had been a major accomplishment to get this far, and it was a relief to have the cold air shut out of the basement. Jerry wanted to concrete the basement at this point, but decided to have it graveled temporarily. He had enough gravel delivered to cover the entire basement floor with several inches. It made the basement a cleaner place to work now that the dirt floor was covered.

Even though the basement area was finally shaping up, Jerry and Suzanne were feeling drained and their morale was low. It seemed like every way they turned, there was some kind of new dilemma. If it wasn't a setback with something in the house, it was the neighborhood or lack of money. Every project had gone over budget. Since Jerry wasn't working a full-time job, and Suzanne's income wasn't enough to cover all of their expenses, they were starting to see a huge problem forming.

They knew that they had taken on more than they could handle, and they weren't getting along anymore. They began to argue about little things frequently. Suzanne cried and prayed at night and Jerry turned the opposite way. He was sure that God had turned His back on him. Since he'd started working day and night on this house, it had become his whole life and consumed him. He wished he'd never laid eyes on it.

Suzanne was sick of living in the filth of construction. They still had no plumbing. Everywhere she looked, there was more work to do. She felt helpless and wanted to give up. There were many days when they could only work on the inside of the house during the winter months. It was cold and bleak outside, which didn't help the dismal mood that had taken over.

Suzanne daydreamed about sunny days and the smell of spring that would soon be in the air. Until then, she knew what she had to look forward to . . . coming home after working all day, pulling up in front of the house, and looking at it with absolute contempt. Her heart felt like it weighed a ton when she looked at it. After everything they'd done, the porch still hadn't been touched yet. It leaned so badly it looked like it wanted to slide right off the house. She often considered driving away from it and never looking back.

The neighbors' houses on either side looked even worse than hers. Suzanne thought about how Gladys' house was peeling paint so badly, it was hard to tell what color it used to be. The screen door was barely hanging on these days. The house on the other side was a rental house, and the family who lived there still had so much junk piled on their porch, Suzanne wondered how they could stand their own filthy surroundings. It seemed like a losing battle, but they were in too deep now, financially and emotionally.

Jerry ate, lived and breathed working on the house, and he had become encapsulated into his own world that revolved around fixing this and fixing that. Some days he acted like he didn't know what to start on first. It was a struggle each day to keep some hope alive.

"Have you got the checkbook with you?" Jerry said over the phone. Suzanne was at work, and he had called when she was, for once, actually sitting at her desk.

"No, I don't have it," Suzanne said as she dug through her purse.

"I think somebody stole it."

"From where?" Suzanne asked, surprised by Jerry's claim. She could hardly believe that his checkbook had been stolen. Jerry was always losing something. Surely he just misplaced it.

"I think somebody stole it out of my truck at the store. They got my wallet, too," he said.

"Oh, hell. Well, we've got to find out. Do you have the phone number from any of the credit card bills? A customer service number or something like that?" Suzanne asked. She rested her forehead on her fist as she talked.

"Wait a minute," Jerry said and put the phone down. Suzanne could hear him digging around in a drawer or something. "Yeah, here's the number to one of them."

Suzanne wrote the number down. "Let me call them to see what I can find out. In the meantime, try to figure out what cards you had in your wallet and call as many as you can, too. I'll call you back in a few minutes."

She hung up and called the customer service number she'd been given. She knew it would be easy to figure out if this one had been stolen and used, since they hadn't purchased anything on it in months. When Suzanne reached a service representative with the credit card company, she was informed that it had been used at several stores in the strip mall across from where Jerry had been parked. About two hundred fifty dollars had been charged in one afternoon on the card. If there had been any doubt that Jerry's wallet and checkbook had been stolen, there wasn't any now.

Suzanne called home. "Yeah, some asshole got your stuff. Do you have phone numbers for any of the other cards that were taken? We have to report them as stolen right away, so we're not responsible for the charges," Suzanne told Jerry.

"Let me call you back. I'm on the other line canceling one now," Jerry said. That day, they reported seven stolen credit cards, including gasoline charge cards, which had hundreds of dollars of charges on them. Jerry also called the bank and put a stop payment on the checks that were taken.

About a week later, Suzanne arrived at work to find a message from Jerry to call him at home. She called him right away, and he informed her that he was on his way to a grocery store, and that some of their stolen checks had shown up along with the thief who was using them. A security guard had detained the man until the police showed up. "They've still got the guy at the store, and the police are there. I'm supposed to go show my ID and identify my checks. Listen, I've got to run. They're waiting for me."

"Call me as soon as you figure out what's going on," Suzanne said. Finally, they would get this joker who took Jerry's things. It was an eerie feeling that someone was using their accounts, looking through Jerry's wallet, surely throwing away any pictures or personal items.

A couple of hours later, Jerry called Suzanne. "You should have seen this jerk. He was rough looking and acted like he was stoned as hell. His eyes were all red and he kept falling asleep, even as he sat there with handcuffs on his wrists. The police wanted to search his car, but he said he rode to the store with somebody. The police looked around out in the parking lot, but I guess whoever drove him there took off when they saw something was up. They kept asking him who he was with, and he wouldn't say. He just kept saying he didn't break into my truck and that he'd found the checks on the side of the road."

"How did they know he was using stolen checks?" Suzanne asked. "I mean, what made them suspicious? Other than the guy's appearance . . ."

"The cashier behind the counter said that the guy had already been in early this morning, around 6:00 a.m. He said he was suspicious because he had the checks wadded up in his pocket and was buying beer early in the morning," Jerry explained. "Then, when the cashier asked for identification, the guy didn't have it, and it was pretty obvious he had stolen the checks. He called the security officer over to hold onto the guy until the police got there."

"I'm glad somebody was paying attention at that store," Suzanne said. For the first time in a long time, she felt like someone was looking out for them.

"Oh, I know… me too. Think about it, Suzanne, this guy passed off about a dozen of my checks all over town, and no one checked for identification. What would really piss me off is if he had gotten away with it. You know what else I found out? The man is already on parole. He's going straight back to jail."

"Jerry, I'm not trying to be superstitious or anything, but it's like ever since we set foot in that house, things just haven't gone right. Doesn't it feel that way to you, too?" Suzanne lowered her voice so she wouldn't be heard by her co-workers. "It feels like we're jinxed or something. I know that having your wallet stolen could happen to anybody, but it just makes me feel like prey. It's as if there's a radar zoned in on us and all the shitty things that could happen, are happening."

"Kind of, yes," Jerry answered with a heavy sigh. He paused for a moment, and Suzanne knew he was thinking about her last statement. She felt compelled to take back what she said.

"Hey, I don't know why I'm talking like this. We won't let all of this get us down, okay? Let's just put it behind us and move on." She knew that he didn't want to dwell on the negativity of their predicament.

"You betcha," Jerry answered wearily. "When you get home, I need to talk to you about some other stuff, too."

When Suzanne got home that afternoon, Jerry informed her that the historic committee was keeping an eye on the improvements being made to the house. "I didn't want to say anything until I knew for sure, but they're making a point of checking up on us. Yesterday, while you were at work, a couple of historic committee officers dropped by to check on the progress we're making on the house. At least that's what they say they're doing. They're friendly enough, but they're scrutinizing the work that's being done."

Suzanne knew that if the historic committee members decided to give them a hard time, their project could be stalled until they complied with any miscellaneous rules they saw fit to enforce, no matter how insignificant the issue.

"They said they've been making themselves more visible in the neighborhood lately… watching rehabs in the district to make sure that historic guidelines are being followed. I understand their position. So, if they zero in on us for any violations, we need to comply with them in a pretty quick manner. We don't want them to pick our house apart; it might get ugly."

"Yeah, but what about the run-down rental houses mixed in with the historic ones? They're exempt from the regulations. And the historic committee is worried that we might put a window in the back of the house that's too modern? Give me a break! If they're going to have an historic overlay in a neighborhood, they should come up with some standards for the houses that are not on the historic homes list, too. Besides, the slum lords who own those places stick occupants in them who bring the whole neighborhood down."

"I know. You're right. Well, we'll play nice with them so they don't give us a hard time. The members of both the historic committee and neighborhood association are teaming up to organize a neighborhood cleanup in a few weeks. They've invited all the folks who live here to participate and pick up trash off the streets. Let's join them in their efforts. It'll show them that we have a genuine interest in preserving the neighborhood, which we do. And hey, it never hurts to schmooze a little."

Jerry called Davis Grey, the event organizer, to volunteer their time for the neighborhood cleanup.

"It's the same year after year. It's the homeowners who meet to help clean up the neighborhood.   Then there are some rental tenants who are so lazy, they sit on their front porch drinking beer and watch while their neighbors pick up trash out of their yards. I'm just telling you this ahead of time, because our turnout for the past two years has practically dwindled away, and that's the reason why," Davis said. "I think this year will be better, though. It seems like the folks who care are starting to outnumber the ones that don't. We'll see you out there. If you have some work gloves, bring them."

A few weeks later, Jerry and Suzanne met about a half-dozen other homeowners and they all set out to pick up trash around the neighborhood. It was a beautiful spring day, and Suzanne felt good just being outside. She filled a large garbage bag full of trash and began filling another one. She felt upbeat, and she was enjoying spending time with Jerry without any arguments to spoil her morning.

Jerry went into the yard of one of the houses to pick up trash. There were a couple of men sitting on the steps of their porch with paper cups and beer cans under their feet. Jerry started to ask the men to excuse him while he picked up the trash, but he thought about it for a second and walked away instead.

"Fuck it," he said to Suzanne when he met back up with her on the street. "If they're too lazy to pick up the trash under their own feet, I'm not going to do it for them!"

Well, there goes my good mood, Suzanne thought.

Chapter 8

Jerry was working in the front yard, raking some of the dirt that had come from the basement. He was preparing it so that he could sew grass seed. As he smoothed the dirt, eyeing it for levelness, he heard a car pull up to the curb behind him. It was an older model Cadillac with an elderly couple in it. Jerry waved and continued to work for a few minutes, but when he saw that the couple was still sitting in their car looking up at the house, he walked toward them and asked, "Can I help you with something?"

The old man rolled his window down and pointed to the house. "I was born there," he said smiling. "I was telling my wife that those steps in front of that house are the same ones in the picture of me when I was a little boy." The old gentleman seemed to look right through Jerry as he took in the sight of his old home place. "I remember playing in the yard and chasing the ice truck up the street." He looked down the street as if he could still see the ice truck driving down the road ahead of him.

"Would you like to come into the house and see it? It's still kind of messy. We're in the process of fixing it up, but you're sure welcome to come in." Jerry motioned toward the house as he spoke.

The old man looked at his wife to get her reaction, and her facial expression was saying no. Respectfully, he declined. "We wouldn't want to put you out."

"It wouldn't be any bother. Really . . ." Jerry gestured to the couple to get out.

He shook his head and refused once again, thanked Jerry and wished him a good day. As the couple slowly drove away, the old man could barely take his eyes off the house long enough to look at the street and drive.

Jerry thought about how many memories there are in his old house. He smiled to think about families living there, kids playing in the yard. He whistled as he went back to work. He felt a genuine sense of accomplishment and was proud of his efforts to save this old family home. He also had a desire to learn more about the history of the house.

Jerry and Suzanne went to the city library and pulled the information about their neighborhood. After scanning through microfiche and old articles that had been filed at the library over the years, they found out that their house had been built, along with the house next to it, by a doctor for his daughters.

The doctor had lived directly across the street in a nice Queen Anne style brick home that was still in excellent shape. The neighbors who lived there now were a hippy-ish couple who seemed to be the free spirits of the neighborhood. They had high ideals and the greatest of intentions, but were the type to talk big and withdraw their efforts quickly in lieu of something better to do to suit their own needs. At least they keep the house up well, Suzanne thought, even if they didn't do anything to improve the neighborhood in general.

"That would be pretty nice," Suzanne said with a sigh.

"What's that?" Jerry asked as he continued looking at the newspaper articles and other information he'd laid out on the library table.

"The doctor who built a house for his children -- what a present," Suzanne said smiling. "Maybe when we're done fixing our house up, we can leave it to our children."

Jerry smiled and nodded as he thumbed through some old photographs. "What children? Don't you have to make children to have children?" He shot a cynical gaze toward Suzanne who purposely ignored him.

In looking at the rest of the papers in front of him, Jerry noted that Cumberland Street, the road their house was built on, had a streetcar that ran through it at the turn of the century. Jerry read this information to Suzanne.

"That explains the wide streets," she said.

"Also, it says here that the alleyways were used for the delivery of coal to each of the houses." He thought back to the large pile of coal that he and Gilbert had taken out of the basement with the wheelbarrow.

"It's hard to believe that our house went from a beautiful bungalow that a doctor built for his daughter to a run-down rental dump used as a crack house," Jerry said as he looked at a picture of the neighborhood that he'd found in an old tax records book.

"Do you think it's worth it? I mean, all this work? Sometimes I wonder," Suzanne said to Jerry as she leaned back in her chair. Her eyes felt a little heavy; it was warm and peaceful in the library. She breathed in deeply, wanting to take the contented feeling home with her.

"It's a little late to ask that question now," Jerry answered dryly.

In an envelope labeled "maps", Jerry found another article about the neighborhood in general. The majority of the district had actually been one huge farm back in the early 1800's. A development company bought the acreage at the turn of the century and began separating the land into residential lots and selling them.

The neighborhood had once been occupied by many professional people including doctors, attorneys, and even a state governor. One of the larger houses had been a funeral home a few decades ago. When the interstate came through the city, it split the neighborhood right in two. As a result, the property values declined and many of the old homes lost their grandeur and succumbed to neglect. Many were condemned and torn down in the 1960's and 1970's.

It was during this time that several plain, distasteful rental duplexes were thrown in on the lots where grand homes had once stood. Property values continued to drop. People were moving to suburbs and outlying towns that were cleaner and newer. The general decline of the neighborhood peaked in the 1980's. That's when investors began purchasing and remodeling some of the houses. After about ten years of spotty rehab projects, the value of the area began to climb somewhat. It seemed that these dinosaurs could shine like new again, and it became chic to own an old house that had been remodeled.

"Who knows? Maybe we bought a diamond in the rough," Jerry said resting his chin on the palm of his hand.

"Maybe," Suzanne said as she gathered the information that was laying on the table. "Let's get out of here. I'm ready to get back to work. If nothing else, this little trip to the library has inspired me."

"Yeah, this was definitely worth doing. It was good to spend some time together without any outside influences."

Chapter 9

"Jesus has been good to me!" Gladys sang. Suzanne looked out the window when she heard this announcement, and saw Gladys standing on her porch singing at the top of her lungs toward the street, her hands raised high toward the sky. The old woman shook her fist and danced a little as she sang, and Suzanne couldn't help but laugh at her even though Gladys' obnoxious singing had become louder and more frequent.

Gladys always had on the wildest looking garbs. Most of the time, she wore three or four mismatched layers of clothes. Today, she was wearing orange and white polyester striped pants and an old, faded green housecoat. Poor old lady, Suzanne thought as she shook her head in pity.

Suzanne tried to ignore the singing and continue working, although she felt edgy as she swept the floor. She wanted to ask Gladys nicely to tone down her voice, but she decided that it was harmless enough, even if it was driving her crazy. Suzanne imagined that she would probably get used to it after awhile.

Lately, it seemed like Gladys was unhappy. Suzanne noticed that she often had a resentful look on her face, and sometimes wouldn't speak when Suzanne or Jerry spoke to her. The only times she appeared friendly was when she wanted something. She had gotten into the habit of coming over and knocking on the door asking for favors. She used a phony-sounding little girl's voice to ask, "Could y'all go pick up a prescription for me?" or "I need to get some groceries, can one of y'all take me to the store?"

Gladys' constant demands were getting old, but Jerry and Suzanne knew she didn't have a car and felt sorry for her, so they tried to help her as much as possible. At first, her son Frank had an old beat-up car, but he was always "out of gas" or gone Lord knows where. A few weeks ago, Frank's car had been repossessed, so he'd started asking Jerry to take him places, too. With all the work to be done, it was a hassle living next to these people.

Suzanne was looking for a pair of pliers and heard a knock at the door. She knew it wasn't Jerry because he was playing basketball at a friend's house. Suzanne cautiously looked around the doorway to see Gladys standing on the porch trying to peer through the window. Suzanne quickly stood back from the entryway, hoping Gladys would think no one was at home. She had put a lace curtain on the window of the front door so that they could avoid being seen when Gladys or her son Frank came to ask for something. Suzanne considered the fact that she needed to put a thicker curtain on the window. After a couple of minutes, Suzanne slowly looked around the doorway again, and Gladys was still standing there. "Good gracious, why won't this lady leave me alone?" she whispered to herself. She felt resentful that she had to hide in her own house from her bothersome neighbor.

A moment later, Suzanne heard Gladys start singing and her voice began trailing off, so she knew that Gladys was walking away from the house. Suzanne breathed a sigh of relief.

Later that afternoon, Suzanne decided to get out of the house for a while and get something to eat. As she stepped out onto her front steps, she heard Gladys' voice. Suzanne thought she was talking to her, so she turned to look at her neighbor.

Gladys was holding her cat like a baby in her arms, talking to it. "Lil' Tom, my neighbor won't help me no more. Naw, she's too busy to come to the door when I need her. I guess she don't wanna be friends no more, huh?"

"Gladys?" Suzanne didn't know whether she should say anything to the woman.

"Don't talk to me, girl! I knew you was at home! I knew, 'cause your truck is parked over there in front of your house. You are a liar." Gladys was still looking at the cat when she spoke, but her voice was much louder.

Suzanne was silent for a moment, surprised to hear Gladys talk this way to her. "I'm sorry, Gladys, I didn't . . ."

"No, ma'am, don't you stand there and tell me a bunch of lies. I don't need you, Suzanne, no more. I don't need your help no more!" She finally raised her head and faced Suzanne. She was frowning and her lips were pressed tightly together.

Suzanne didn't answer. She continued to her truck and drove to the next street. She pulled over and took a deep breath to calm her nerves. Oh, brother, this is not a good situation, she thought.

Jerry and Suzanne started parking their vehicles in the backyard via the alley and coming in through the back door to avoid being seen by Gladys, who was usually sitting on her front porch. This worked most of the time, but occasionally Gladys was standing in her back yard when they came home. Suzanne was especially careful not to pay attention to Gladys as she walked past her.

"Jerry, can you take me to the store to cash a check?" Gladys said as she walked down the steps at the back of her house.

Jerry was surprised that she was asking him for a favor after the argument she'd tried to start with Suzanne. "Uh, I need to go into the house for a minute first. I'll be back out in a minute."

"Suzanne, Gladys is out here asking me to take her to the store. Did you two kiss and make up?"

Suzanne was standing in the kitchen drinking water. She almost choked on it. "No, I haven't spoken to her since the day she was fussing at me."

"Well, I guess she's only mad at you because she's still bugging me to do stuff for her."

"Better you than me!" Suzanne laughed.

Gradually, Gladys started coming around to being civil to Suzanne again. She began by waving hello one afternoon when Suzanne went out onto her porch. She waved back and kept walking. Then Gladys said "hi" to her. It wasn't long before she had the nerve to ask Suzanne to pick up a prescription for her. In her desire to cultivate good will with her neighbor, she agreed. It started to become a habit again.

Suzanne was aggravated that she had to sneak out of her own house to go anywhere, but avoidance was the only way she could escape from driving Gladys someplace. Suzanne began to feel unappreciated as Gladys seemed to expect her to drop everything and take her to run errands. It wasn't just the inconvenience. The old woman smelled so bad that Suzanne's truck stunk like body odor and stale cigarette smoke when she got out. But the worst part was the uneasy feeling Suzanne had around Gladys. She frequently seemed discontented and irritable. Her sour mood was more than her mental illness emerging out of her; it seemed like a sense of resentment toward her new neighbors.

Jerry continued to work on the rewiring of the electrical system in between working on other projects throughout the house. Sometimes he didn't know how to prioritize since there were so many things to be done. The wiring had proved to be a much harder job than he'd anticipated. Unlike new construction where the wiring could be routed through the walls with little or no hindrance, coercing it through the walls in this house was quite a challenge. The studs weren't always spaced evenly and of course there was the drywall to contend with.

Jerry was at one end of a circuit, trying to fish a wire through the wall to Suzanne so that she could pull it through an outlet hole. He'd attached it to a "snake" that was designed for running electrical wiring through walls.

The snake had gotten caught up in the wall and it wouldn't budge either way. Jerry cussed the wiring. "Goddamn it, get through there, you mother-fucker!" Sweat was dripping from his forehead, nose and chin. Suzanne anxiously peered into the hole in the wall looking for the end of the wire to appear.

"It's not showing up yet," Suzanne said.

"I know!" Jerry snapped. "The son-of-a-bitch is stuck!"

The wiring would prove to be a sore spot for as long as they worked on the house. Jerry knew that he'd have to take a test to prove his knowledge of wiring before codes would approve it. He hoped as he worked his way through the wiring of the house using do-it-yourself wiring manuals that he'd learn enough to be able to pass the test.

Suzanne's father Paul pulled up to the curb in front of Suzanne's house. He had come to help with some of the projects that were going on. Since the death of his wife, he had plenty of time on his hands and was glad to get out of his house and do something with his time. As he walked up the sidewalk toward the house, he wondered what the mood would be like today. He'd noticed that when he came to Jerry and Suzanne's house lately that there was a lot of anxiety. Jerry's language had become vulgar and he was short tempered. Suzanne also seemed impatient and unhappy.

Paul also observed a growing sense of urgency at getting some of the projects done. He knew that the funding for the renovation had mostly come from Jerry's parents. The way Suzanne had explained it to him, they forwarded money to

Jerry when he requested it, and they kept a running total of what was owed. They also allowed Jerry to use their credit card for miscellaneous expenses and food. Without their financial support, Jerry and Suzanne's work couldn't have been done. Paul worried that Suzanne was already way over her head in debt to Jerry's parents, and that all the hours she was putting in at the house and at her job would start seriously affecting her physically.

When Paul knocked on the door, Suzanne answered it with a hammer in her hand. "Whoa, watch where you swing that thing!" he teased as he raised his hands in mock defense.

"Ha ha ha," Suzanne said sarcastically.

"So kiddo, what are you tearing up today?" He hugged her and entered the house. The front room was a mess with boards and building supplies laying everywhere. Suzanne looked worn-out, but seemed glad to see her father. "Where's Jerry?"

"Oh, he's working on the breaker box in the back of the house." Suzanne pointed with the hammer she was still holding. "Here, have a seat. I've got to rest for a little while. We've been working on the wiring since seven o'clock this morning." Suzanne took a bucket of nails off a chair and motioned for her father to sit. She sat on a toolbox nearby and sipped on some bottled water.

"Suzanne, I'm really worried about you and Jerry. Seriously, you two look beat. I want to help. Let me know what I can do."

"Daddy, the house is already way over-budget, and I'm going to have to get a loan to pay taxes and some other bills that have come due. Jerry even had to use the inheritance from his brother who died last year to help make ends meet around here. I feel like we've exhausted all of the money that we dare to take from Jerry's parents. They still offer more, but Daddy, we have to pay that back, and right now, that looks impossible."

"Well, you've come this far. I know that it feels like you'll never get done with this place, but you will. Don't lose hope, okay?" He got up from the chair and hugged his daughter. She felt small and fragile in his embrace as she began to cry into his shoulder.

"The house still feels so unstable. Jerry's mad all the time, and I'm tired of living in dirt." Suzanne sobbed. Her father held her while she cried it out. He knew his daughter was upset and tired, but he knew that she was strong enough to handle this situation she'd gotten herself into.

"Suzanne, don't worry. We will finish this house. All of us together can get this done."

Chapter 10

Suzanne found herself calling and chewing out some of the contractors who had been hired to help with the house projects. Why couldn't these guys keep their appointments? Suzanne thought. And if they couldn't make it to their appointments, why couldn't they call and let anyone know?

Suzanne felt hot as she dialed the number for the roofers who were supposed to replace the shingles on the sides of the house. When the answering machine picked up, Suzanne paused before she spoke, trying to steady her voice. "Gary, this is Suzanne. I talked to you last week, and you were supposed to start on our roof today. I just got home from work, and you didn't show up! No phone call, nothing. Listen, I got your name from a friend of mine. If this is the sloppy way you do your business, I'll make sure she knows not to recommend you to anyone else." Suzanne's mouth was dry as she hung up the phone.

Within minutes, the phone rang and Suzanne, who hadn't moved from her position by the phone, answered it quickly.

"Suzanne? This is Gary. I'm calling you back to say I'm really sorry for not showing up today. Listen, I know you're mad, but I got hung up on another job and couldn't make it. You're right, I should've called."

"Well, I understand. I'm sorry I was so upset when I left that message, but you have no idea what we've had to deal with here. You're just one of several contractors who've done this to us, and I was pretty ticked off about it."

"No, I'm the one who should apologize. If you still want us to do the work, I can get a crew out there tomorrow. It's up to you. And no matter what you decide, I'll understand."

Suzanne felt like some kind of monster with this guy apologizing to her. "Yeah, that would be good. I appreciate you calling me back so quickly."

"We'll see you tomorrow. I just hope you're not still mad at me and try to beat me up." Gary laughed.

Suzanne laughed, too, but she wasn't amused.

The next morning, Suzanne's phone rang at work. "Hey, how's it going so far today?" Jerry asked.

"Oh, pretty good, I guess. Did the roofers show up yet?"

"Yes, they're setting up right now. Nice guys, I think you'll like them. Robbie's here, too, believe it or not. Listen, I really called to tell you that I just got in an argument with Gladys. I was working with Robbie on the side of the house, and she came out on her porch and yelled at us, saying we're stealing her water."

"What? Stealing her water? That doesn't even make sense," Suzanne said.

"I must have stood there for ten minutes telling her that there's no way we could be stealing her water. At least I tried to tell her. She would hardly let me get a word in edgewise. She said she saw water trickling out of our hose spigot under the house and that her last water bill was over eighty dollars. She's convinced we're stealing her water, and nothing I said made things any better."

"Did you tell her we don't even have any plumbing in the house yet?" Suzanne asked.

"Yes, I did. But that didn't seem to mean much to her. She also kept saying that all this digging we're doing for the foundation is flooding her basement, and that we're killing the tree in her front yard by chopping the roots. Suzanne, I think she's lost it." Jerry sounded out of breath. "I finally just stopped trying to talk to her about it and walked away. She just kept saying 'I know y'all are stealing my water, Jerry'. She said that God was watching us and that he'll make us sorry for what we're doing to her. Oh, and she came up with some pretty creative names to call me."

"What kind of names? Nevermind, I don't want to know. Just please don't talk to her anymore about it. If she says anything else to you, ignore her. Just be nice to her and hopefully this will blow over soon. You know how she is, mad one minute and asking for something the next."

"I'm as nice as she'll let me be. By the way, the roofers thought it was a pretty good show. I saw them looking at each other when Gladys was out there hollering at me."

Suzanne hung up the phone and tried to concentrate on her work, but she couldn't help but worry about what was going on at home. She felt uneasy about the whole situation with Gladys. It was more than just a bad feeling that things had turned hostile between the neighbors. It felt like a prophecy of things to come.

Gladys' singing had become a nuisance. It was more frequent and louder than ever. With the houses being so close together, there was no escaping it. At this point, it wasn't even singing anymore; it was wailing, and her voice became hoarse after several hours.

Suzanne felt her relationship with Gladys declining with each day that passed. Along with the miserable singing episodes, she often went out on her porch and preached the gospel as well. She lectured to the streets with her arms held out. "Jesus is good. Lord Almighty!" she hollered. Sometimes she looked dazed as she paced back and forth on her porch, echoing her sermons to the world, pointing at imaginary parishioners.

If he'd sit and listen, Gladys would also preach to her son. He didn't appear to be looking at her when she'd tell him that the Lord didn't approve of the things he was doing. His posture was often slumped over, looking at the uneven boards of the porch. Other times, he simply looked toward the street with no outward emotion.

Some days, her screaming tirades began in the morning and didn't end until nighttime. Even when it was cold outside, she wrapped herself in an old blanket and went out on the porch to preach and sing.

"She's about to drive me nuts with this. I know she's mad at us because she thinks we're stealing from her, but to be this vocal day and night -- it's too much. I wish she'd just do her caterwauling in her house. At least that would muffle it some," Suzanne said to Jerry one afternoon after trying to tune it out.

"First of all, she's probably like this regardless of who lives next door. But I do think she's cranked it up a few notches to get to us. I'm not going to give her the satisfaction. I'll just go about my business like usual."

Jerry's friend Bill came to visit from Connecticut. Jerry had been looking forward to his visit for weeks. As Bill walked up the sidewalk toward Jerry's house, he turned to see Gladys glaring at him from her porch next door. She had curlers sloppily piled on the top of her head, with strands of hair sticking out, and she was leaning over resting her arm on her cane.

Bill looked at the ground to shake off the old woman's scowling face only to look back up and see her still staring a hole through him. He took his hand out of his pocket to wave hello, but her voice stopped him cold.

"Don't you park in front of my house," she growled. Her eyes narrowed, and she straightened up in her chair. "You better move your car, Mister." Her voice sounded angry, and Bill wondered why she was being so vicious. He picked up his pace and kept walking, careful not to look back at her as he walked up to Jerry's house.

He knocked on the door. "Hey, buddy! Come on in!" Jerry said as he patted Bill on the back.

As soon as Bill stepped inside, he pointed toward Gladys' house and said, "Oh God, that's what you've been telling me about."

"Yep. That's it," Jerry said. "We're about to go bananas being around her."

"I can see what you mean. She gave me some nasty looks. I'll bet nobody wants to come over here to visit you guys with that mean old woman living next door. Hey, we better get on out of here and go to dinner. She already said I better move my car. She says I'm parked in front of her house."

"Oh, she decided to show off her hospitable nature to you, huh?" Jerry laughed. "If that was all we had to deal with, that would be a dream. She never shuts up. But that's a long story. I'll tell you about it over dinner."

Chapter 11

"You guys ought to join the neighborhood association," a gentleman said as he placed a folded piece of paper under the flag of Jerry and Suzanne's mailbox.

Jerry was cleaning some tools in the front yard. He stood up and walked toward the man who had spoken to him.

"I'm Chris Miller, the neighborhood association president, at least for the rest of the year." He held out his hand to shake Jerry's.

"It's good to meet you. I'll discuss it with my wife. It would probably be a good thing to meet more of our neighbors. I'm afraid we've been so wrapped up with all of our projects that we just haven't gotten out to mingle with anyone."

"Neighborhood meetings are held the second Tuesday of every month unless otherwise noted in one of these newsletters." He held up the stack of folded flyers that he hadn't delivered yet.

"Sounds good. By the way, I'm Jerry and my wife is Suzanne."

"I know." Chris smiled as he waved goodbye and walked down the street.

Jerry decided to take a break for lunch and joined Suzanne in the kitchen. "What do you think about joining the neighborhood association? The president of the association just walked past the house handing out newsletters, and he invited us to go to their meeting."

Suzanne thought about it for a moment. Maybe they could get moral support from other people in the neighborhood who had been living there for a long time. Maybe these neighbors could even shed some light on how to get along with Gladys. It had gotten to the point where the constant singing and wild accusations were getting under their skin. If nothing else, they could use some new friends.

"You know, that's not a bad idea. I've never been involved in anything like that. It sounds pretty fun."

Jerry and Suzanne went to the next meeting which was held at one of the larger, statelier homes in the neighborhood. Suzanne was excited to finally have a reason to see the inside of it. She wasn't disappointed. The entryway was dramatic with an arched doorway that must have been twelve feet tall with elaborate cut glass windows. As they approached the front door, the light from inside of the house danced between the panes of glass. Before they could knock, the door opened and a large gentleman with a beard smiled and ushered them inside. The meeting was already underway, so they found a seat close to the door and sat quietly while the people in the room discussed various issues.

Many topics of discussion sounded trivial to Suzanne, but she listened with feigned interest and stifled several yawns. After listening to one of the men drone on and on about someone knocking his garbage cans over in the alley, the gentleman who let them in the house announced that the meeting had been adjourned, and that there were refreshments in the dining room.

Jerry and Suzanne decided to stay and meet some of the other people in attendance of the meeting. Suzanne noticed that everyone seemed to know each other pretty well. There were small groups of three or four people standing around talking quietly. From some area of the house that she couldn't pinpoint, soft piano music had filled the room to the point that she couldn't hear any of the discussions that were going on. She felt awkward as she drank coffee and smiled at anyone who looked at her.

"So, you're the folks who bought the house down there next to the singer," said a nice looking man with glasses and a turtleneck. He held out his hand. "I'm Jack Miller. I don't think I know your names."

Suzanne shook his hand, and thought how soft it felt. "I'm Suzanne Peters, and that's my husband Jerry."

Chris Miller walked up to join the two in discussion. He was wearing a baseball cap with a beer logo on it. It seemed out of place on his head. "Suzanne, I'm Chris. I met your husband a few days ago. I wanted to let you know how happy we are that you bought that old house. Man, that's a lot of work! I walked around in that old thing when it went up for sale, and I couldn't imagine trying to get that place fixed up. You're brave, lady!" He smiled and patted her on the shoulder.

"Well, I don't know if you'd say that we're brave or just plain stupid."

Chris and Jack both laughed politely and appeared fascinated in what she had to say.

"It's been a long journey to this point, but I have to admit, now that we're finally meeting some other people in the neighborhood, I'm starting to feel a little better about things."

"Oh, have you had any problems? Except for all the hard work, I mean," said Jack.

Suzanne smiled sarcastically. "Well, sometimes we feel like we're fighting a losing battle with our neighbor," she explained to the men. "Maybe you can give us some advice on how to deal with Gladys next door. Both of you know her, right?"

The men looked at each other and then looked at Suzanne and chuckled.

"Yes, you have a problem on your hands. She's schizophrenic, I think." Chris adjusted his clipboard as he talked. "She has a history of acting bizarre. Her husband recently died. He was a lot older than her." Chris asked Jack, "Do you remember when she ran out of her house and down the block screaming, saying that her husband was trying to stab her with a butcher knife?"

Jack nodded. "She's been in and out of mental hospitals. Her husband used to commit her and she'd be gone for months at a time. She'd get out and things would be quiet for awhile, then it would start up all over again."

"Her son, Frank, has also had some problems. He got kicked out of school for something, but nobody knows why. He tried to join the Army, but he was turned down. Again, nobody really knows what that was all about. I'm not so sure they tell the truth about things. I suppose it's really none of our business, but one can't help but wonder," Chris said.

"I feel sorry for them. I know they're having a hard time in life. But they're making us miserable. We've done everything we can think of to get along with them, and it's never enough," Suzanne said with more emotion than she meant to show. "We've put everything we've got, financially, physically and mentally, into our house, and we just want some peace."

Jack took a drink and shook his head. "I wouldn't want to live next to them. That's all I can say. Honey, if you ever feel threatened, don't you hesitate to call the police. Or you can always call me." He looked into her eyes with such intensity that it made her intentionally look away.

"Why don't we bring it up at the next neighborhood meeting and see if anybody has any suggestions," Chris said as he put on his jacket. "If we can help, let us know."

A woman with a large plate of food walked up to the group. "You talking about your favorite neighbor?" she asked as she stuffed a potato chip in her mouth. "By the way, I'm Vergie. I live on the other side of Gladys."

"It's nice to meet you," Suzanne answered. She suddenly wanted to change the subject. Actually, she wanted to leave, but she felt obligated to be social as she turned to the woman with a smile.

"Well, I'm mad at her," Vergie said as she wiped her face with a napkin.

"Oh, really?" Suzanne answered.

"Yeah, either she or her son put broken glass under my fence to cut my little dog Captain. When Frank goes out there, Captain runs along the fence 'cause he wants to play with him. Next thing I know, there's big pieces of broken glass, looks like broken soda bottles, crammed all along the bottom of the fence. I had to put on my gardening gloves and dig it all out with a spade. Now, I don't know which one of them did it, but it didn't sit too well with me," she said in an agitated voice.

Suzanne wanted to back up as Vergie kept inching closer to her as she spoke. It made her uncomfortable, and the woman smelled like onion dip.

"If they keep doing that to your dog, call the police about it. I don't know what else you can do," Suzanne answered. "I wouldn't let them get away with it, though."

Vergie pursed her lips and stared at Suzanne hard. "No, I'll just go over there and kick their asses next time they do that."

Suzanne suspected Vergie had more to drink that night than the punch she was holding in her hand. She also knew that she was just wasting her breath talking to this woman. She didn't doubt that Vergie could kick anyone's ass; she was a sizable woman who looked masculine in her flannel shirt and boots. But she felt that no one was going to take any real action except her husband and herself.

Suzanne and Jerry walked home from the meeting thinking about conversations they'd had with new acquaintances.

"I'm going to read up on schizophrenia. That's what Chris said Gladys has. If we learn more about it, we can handle the situation better. Maybe there's something we haven't thought of yet that would help us get along with her. Then maybe we can have some harmony around here," Suzanne said as they stepped onto their front porch. She looked next door and studied the darkness. She didn't know what she was looking for, but she had a feeling of uneasiness.

Suzanne began reading everything she could regarding schizophrenia. She read books from the library and articles from the Internet. Her need to put a bandage on the situation had become so strong that she was obsessed with finding out as much information as possible.

One article on the Internet was particularly interesting. There was a checklist of symptoms and descriptions of classic schizophrenia traits. Distrust or suspiciousness was at the top of the list. One thing is for sure, Suzanne thought, that's definitely a good description of Gladys. She read the other symptoms -- delusions or hallucinations, bizarre behavior, decreased speech or lack of emotion. Suzanne had noticed all of these in Gladys' personality. She printed the article and took it home.

"Fidgeting; pacing or hyperactivity; compulsive rituals . . . Jerry, these descriptions all fit Gladys. Listen, here are some more -- poor grooming and social inabilities," Suzanne read aloud.

"All of that sounds just like her. She can't hold a normal conversation. Her emotions and responses don't seem to be appropriate to the conversation at hand and you know how she sometimes stares off in space when someone's talking to her," Jerry said, processing the information Suzanne was reading.

"It also says here that people with paranoid schizophrenia hear voices. Think about how many times she's used God as her defense in a situation where she was losing control. She believes she's being spoken to directly by God, and that she's above everyone else because He favors her."

Some of the information Suzanne read about schizophrenia mentioned that getting along with people who had the affliction was often difficult, and at times little or no provocation was needed to bring on an outburst. No kidding, Suzanne thought.

"At least now we know what we're dealing with," Suzanne said. "But how do we get along with her? She's so mean spirited."

"I'll do what I can to get along with her, but I'm not walking on eggshells all the time, I can tell you that."

"Jerry, I just don't trust the woman. All those veiled threats about God watching us and that He'll make us sorry for what we've done to her . . . Disease or no disease, I'm tired of the way she treats us. Just looking over toward her house makes me feel uncomfortable, almost like I'm starting a fight if I so much as glance in that direction. There's got to be a way to make this situation better."

Suzanne decided to try to contact Gladys' doctor. Gladys had mentioned on several occasions the name of the mental hospital where she had been a patient. Suzanne had seen the doctor's name on the prescription bottles she used to pick up for her.

"They'll never talk to you about her," Jerry warned. "You probably won't even get them to acknowledge her as a patient."

Suzanne decided to call the mental health clinic anyway, despite what Jerry said. "Well, they can tell me to buzz off when I call, but here goes nothing."

When the receptionist answered the phone, Suzanne explained that she knew Gladys was a patient at the clinic and wanted to discuss a serious situation with her doctor. To Suzanne's total amazement, the receptionist put her through to the doctor.

"Hello, this is Dr. Singh, can I help you?" said a voice with an Indian accent.

Suzanne took a breath, trying to figure out the best way to approach the doctor with their problem. She felt nervous as she spoke. "Yes, hello, my name is Suzanne, and I'm a neighbor of Gladys Grubb, one of your patients. We've lived next door to her for a while now, and we just thought you should know that she may be having some difficulties living on her own," Suzanne said. She was so anxious to get her words out and so surprised that the doctor was willing to listen to her that she didn't stop to let the doctor respond. "She acts so aggressively that it seems she's not in control of herself sometimes. We feel like we've tried everything to get along with her. We've tried ignoring her, but she's very vocal and abusive. How can anyone ignore someone like that?" Suzanne felt her throat tighten with emotion. She finally took another breath and tried to calm herself down. Suzanne realized she was shaking.

The doctor hesitated before answering. "I'm sorry. I cannot give you any information as to whether or not she is my patient. All I can tell you is that if you fear that your neighbor is a threat to herself or others, call the police. A person cannot be committed unless they do something dangerous or if the person's family takes it upon themselves to admit them to a mental hospital. Beyond that, I cannot discuss anything with you. I'm truly sorry."

"I realize you can't tell me anything, but please just listen, it seems like she's having issues with managing her anger. She hasn't done anything violent yet, that we know of, but what I'm trying to say is that we don't know what she's capable of doing."

The doctor was silent. Suzanne waited expectedly, listening intently for a response from her. She didn't get one.

Wondering if she should match the doctor's silence with her own or if she should say something, Suzanne started to ask a question, but was interrupted by the doctor.

"Ma'am, I'm sure it's difficult to live so close to someone who has outbursts like the ones you're describing. People who have mental illnesses are hard to control even in a hospital environment. The only thing I can do is give you the emergency number to call if your neighbor has another emotional occurrence where you think she may be a danger to herself or others. Don't hesitate to call it. It's the direct number to the mental health crisis mobile unit. They're on call seven days a week, twenty-four hours per day."

The doctor gave Suzanne the number and thanked her for calling, telling her "good luck". Suzanne felt better for having talked to her, even if she couldn't discuss the situation openly.

Suzanne decided to follow up with Vergie on the short conversation they had at the neighborhood meeting. She knocked on Vergie's door and heard a dog barking inside. She waited a few minutes before turning to leave. She must not be home, Suzanne thought. She walked down the steps, disappointed that she didn't get a chance to talk to Vergie.

The door opened, and Vergie stuck her head out. "Well, hello. Suzanne, right?"

"Yeah, that's me." Suzanne smiled as she walked back up the steps to the front door. "Do you have a minute? I wanted to talk to you about you-know-who." She motioned with her eyes toward Gladys' house. "You've been here for a long time, and somehow you've survived it. I just need to talk to someone who knows what we're trying to come to grips with over here."

"Well, sure. Come on in. Ignore this dirty house. My kids just come in from school and lay their stuff everywhere. The dog won't bite; he just likes to bark when people come over." Vergie removed a backpack from one of the living room chairs. "Here, have a seat. Want something to drink?"

"No, no, I'm fine. I just thought it was time we had a visit and talked about things. Like I said, I need your help in figuring out how to handle Gladys. I have a feeling that it's going to get worse before it gets better, and obviously, you're still living next to her, so you must be doing something that I'm not as far as being able to get along with her."

"Well, first of all we don't get along with each other. I don't speak to the woman. She's given me a hard time about several things since I moved in here thirteen years ago."

Suzanne shifted in her seat. It was uncomfortable, and one of the springs was sticking her in the behind.

"I've been hoping her family would commit her for several years now, but they haven't done it yet; at least not permanently. She's pretty crazy acting sometimes." Vergie lit a cigarette. "Do you mind if I smoke?"

"No, go ahead. That's okay," Suzanne said shaking her head.

"Her husband used to commit her every so often when he couldn't handle her any more, but she was always out within a few weeks. I think once she stayed in for almost a year. But since he died, no one in that family will take responsibility for her. I've spoken to her son, her daughter, and her stepdaughter. It seems to me that they're not interested in helping her. One of the biggest problems is that she won't take her medicine."

Suzanne stared at the smoldering cigarette that was in the ash tray next to Vergie. "What can we do? I mean, we're being forced every day to listen to her singing, preaching, and threats. It's gotten so that we do everything possible to avoid being in our own yard. But it doesn't stop there. As I know you're aware, because our houses are so close together, we can hear her from inside the house, too. There's no escaping the noise. Little things like taking a nap, we never get to do that no matter how tired we are. And friends don't like to visit because she hollers at them as they walk up to our house."

Vergie listened and nodded. She waved her hand to shoo away a fly that was bothering her.

"Honey, I know exactly what you're going through. All of those things happen to us, too. It drives my kids nuts."

"We park in the back yard so we can avoid her glaring at us from her front porch when we come home. We worry about the house when we leave. Who knows what she might do while we're gone?"

"Here are your options. You can either put up with it or find another place to live. I'm a single mother with two kids. I can't afford to move. So, I just manage to deal with it. It's not easy, believe me, but after all this time, it's almost a matter of principle to me now. She's not going to make me sell my house and put my finances in jeopardy. She's just not worth it. I wish I could give you some advice that would make this situation easier for you, but the fact is I can't."

Suzanne thanked Vergie and got up to leave. "I'm glad we had some time to visit. I enjoyed talking to you."

Vergie patted her on the shoulder, "You'll be alright. If anything happens and you need me, you just come on over here and get me, you hear?"

The next day was Saturday, and it started out with brilliant sunlight and singing birds. Suzanne wanted to get an early start and decided she'd finish working on the claw foot bathtub. She'd already sanded off most of the multiple layers of paint from the outside of the tub the weekend before.

Jerry helped her get prepped for finishing the job by laying the tub on its side on the front porch. Suzanne was setting up the sander when the screen door creaked open and slammed shut next door. The smell of cigarette smoke drifted through the air. They looked at each other, bracing for what they knew was coming.

Suzanne could see Gladys walk across her porch out of the corner of her eye. She sat on her green lounge chair facing the street with a cigarette in her hand. Suzanne felt tense with anticipation of another confrontation with her neighbor.

Gladys waited for a few minutes before speaking. Her voice was raspy, but plenty audible. "You people think you can do whatever you want over there. You think you can steal my water and tear up my yard. You're trying to run me off. I've been here twenty years, and I ain't going nowhere. You hear me?"

Suzanne didn't answer her. What could she say in response to the woman's ramblings?

Gladys continued, "My water bill was over eighty dollars last month and you're trying to kill my tree. I can't get no sun; I've got a disease and the sun would kill me, and now you're trying to kill my tree."

Suzanne thought it was unnerving, but she kept busy digging for sandpaper in a box that was sitting on the porch. She glanced at Gladys as she stood from the box of supplies. Gladys' frizzy gray hair was combed straight up, and she looked like a fat troll. As she continued to talk, she became more animated. Suzanne couldn't see her face completely, but could tell that she was frowning as she began gesturing with her hands as she talked. She was repeating phrases, "Y'all ain't going to run me off. You're the ones that's going to leave. You fools, nasty asses . . . You're going to learn you can't run over people and steal their water."

Suzanne pretended to ignore her. She had a sinking feeling because she knew she couldn't avoid this behavior forever. Her hands were shaking as she leaned against the tub. She started sanding, purposely paying close attention to her project.

Once Gladys realized that she wasn't affecting anyone with her comments, she raised her voice and yelled, "Jerry, I know what you're trying to do to me, and it ain't going to work!" She continued her rant, putting out her cigarette. "I ain't scared of you! I'll make sure you know I mean business."

Jerry looked over to see Gladys turn around to face him. She was getting worked up and was breathing heavy. There was pure hatred in her eyes.

This was getting old. Suzanne fought to hold her anger in. She was being bullied, and she didn't like it. Finally, Suzanne couldn't be quiet any longer. "Jerry, don't listen to her. She sounds like a broken record." She waved her hand toward Gladys, dismissing her incoherent chatter. Then she said in an elevated voice so Gladys could hear her, "She's trying to get to us. Just ignore her."

"Suzanne, you go to hell!" Gladys said narrowing her eyes. Her voice was gravelly, and it sounded like a growl.

"Now, what kind of way is that to talk for a Christian like you? I thought you were such a Christian!" Suzanne answered, emphasizing the word Christian in a sarcastic tone. She couldn't remember the last time she raised her voice to anyone. It felt strange. The words seemed to force themselves out of her mouth.

"I am a Christian, and you're going to hell, Suzanne," Gladys snapped. Her voice echoed down the street. Gladys furrowed her eyebrows as she glared with loathing.

Suzanne put her tools down on the porch and turned to step into her house. "Jerry, I'm not listening to this crazy stuff anymore. I'm going back inside for awhile. You can stay out here, or you can come in, too. That's up to you."

"I'm not crazy, Suzanne, you are," Gladys said, her voice exploding with anger. She turned back around and sat in her lounge chair, sulking, muttering to herself. They couldn't understand everything she was saying, but they made out words and phrases . . . hate them people, think they can come in here and do what they want to, stealin' my water.

"Gladys, how many times are we going to talk about this water thing? We don't have any plumbing in the house yet. We get water from their hose next door." Jerry pointed to the house on the other side of his. It was as if he was talking to a child. He felt silly because she wasn't even looking at him while he spoke.

Suzanne stopped to listen to the conversation. She didn't want to leave Jerry alone to defend himself against Gladys' accusations.

"I see that water dripping under your porch. You are, too, stealing my water," Gladys said. She was now facing the opposite direction, but she turned her head over her shoulder to shout.

"That's the stupidest thing I've ever heard," Suzanne said, her own voice beginning to match the volume of her neighbor's. She felt her resolve melting away.

Gladys cut her off. "And Suzanne, your mama was crazy -- crazy for having you!" Her eyes were wild as she turned her head around on her fat neck to face Suzanne. Her hair was out of control and her lips were drawn back in a scowl showing her yellowed teeth.

Suzanne was disgusted and stood on her porch feeling speechless. She could see she was getting nowhere arguing with Gladys. The old woman was convinced that she was a victim.

"Let's get out of here," Suzanne said to Jerry. "We've got to let things cool off here for awhile. Let's go get lunch or something. She can sit there and feel sorry for herself all damned day for all I care."

Chapter 12

Finally, the foundation was finished and the floors were level. Oak flooring was delivered to be installed throughout the main level of the house. Jerry hired an old friend of his that he worked with at a hardwood flooring company to do the installation. Marvin Perry was skilled at installing tongue-in-groove hardwood floors. His method was fast, and he was such a big guy that he covered a lot of territory in a short time with his accurate and firm hits to the hydraulic nail gun. He'd been down on his luck lately due to a disagreement he had with his previous employer and was grateful to get the job. Marvin was the brother of Robbie Perry, who had been working on the foundation.

The first day Marvin was expected to show up to work on the floors at 9:00 a.m. Jerry called Suzanne at work around lunchtime.

"How's it going? Is Marvin there yet?" Suzanne asked.

"Nope," Jerry said.

"Where is his sorry ass? Did he call?" Suzanne was already feeling the familiar disappointment that she had become accustomed to during this house project. She had a feeling that he wouldn't show up on time, yet she was still surprised that he didn't.

"Nope," Jerry answered.

"We've got to get those floors done or we can't do anything else! Does Robbie know where he is?" Suzanne asked.

"Robbie didn't show either," Jerry said flatly.

"This is fucked up, you know that?" Suzanne said. "Well, we've got to get in touch with Marvin. He's got to get to work on those floors."

"I'll leave him a message," Jerry said.

The next day, Marvin showed up around eleven o'clock with no tools.

"Where are your tools?" Jerry asked looking behind Marvin's large frame at his van parked in front of the house.

"Well, that's what I need to talk to you about, Jerry," Marvin explained as he stepped into the front door, "I had to sell them." He thumped the cigarette that he was smoking out the front door into the yard before closing the door. His voice was calm, but he was sweating.

"You sold them? Well, how are you going to work on these floors?" Jerry asked. "Why did you sell them?"

"I had to pay a guy some money for some stuff I stole from him," Marvin looked at the floor while he was talking to Jerry. He wiped his forehead with the back of his hand.

Jerry felt helpless and aggravated. He took a minute to compose his thoughts before he spoke again.

"Where are the tools now?" Jerry asked. He had his hands on his hips and it was all he could do to keep from shaking Marvin.

"They're at the pawn shop down the road," he said without looking up from the floor.

"Let's go get them," Jerry said as he pushed him aside to open the door. Marvin followed behind him like a scolded child, saying nothing.

They went to the pawnshop, and Jerry paid to get the tools out of hock. Upon returning to the house, Marvin started laying out the boards and Jerry went to get both of them some lunch. They ate mostly in silence, only speaking when necessary. For the remainder of the day, Jerry forced himself to be civil, but wasn't friendly.

After working several hours, Marvin had almost finished laying the flooring in two rooms. "Good job, Buddy!" Jerry said and shook his hand. "What time are you going to be here tomorrow?" He was feeling better about the situation, and was genuinely happy with the results of the floor so far. He even felt a little guilty for his cold demeanor all day.

"I'll be here around nine-thirty," Marvin said as he packed up the tools to leave.

The next morning, Marvin showed up around eleven o'clock. He got to work immediately and finished the two rooms he'd started the day before. He then began working on the kitchen floor. He'd gotten about three-quarters of the way through the kitchen and said he had to go home and go to the bathroom. Marvin lived all the way on the other side of town.

"You've got to be kidding me," Jerry said and laughed. "There's a bathroom right down the street at that fast food place. That's where we have to go all the time."

"No, I can't go in a public place. I have to go home." Marvin shook his head. He hurriedly gathered his tools. He didn't act as if he thought the situation was humorous at all. "I'll be back in about an hour."

Jerry thought it was funny that a big guy like Marvin was so modest about his bathroom habits. He laughed to think about Marvin driving all the way home to go "number two".

Marvin didn't return to work that afternoon. Jerry called his house and paged him, but he couldn't be reached. I should've never let him leave this house with those tools, he thought. He was upset with himself for being so gullible.

When Suzanne got home from work, Jerry was sitting on the floor, sawing the bottom of a doorjamb back to accommodate the new flooring. "Where's Marvin?" she asked.

"He went home to take a shit and never came back," Jerry said as he sat up and leaned against the doorway to rest for a moment.

"Oh, Lord, I've heard it all now," Suzanne said as she threw her purse into a nearby chair. She sat on the floor next to Jerry. "What's his number? I'm calling that fat bastard now. Don't worry, I'll be nice."

Jerry got up and dug through his wallet to find Marvin's number. Suzanne was exasperated as she dialed the phone. When the answering machine picked up, Suzanne started out calm, "Hi, Marvin, this is Suzanne. You didn't come back to work on the floors when you left for lunch." She could feel her anger beginning to choke her. "You better get your ass over here tomorrow and finish the job that we've paid you to do. You screw over all your friends who try to help you and then you wonder why nobody cares about you. Give us a call tonight, you asshole!" Suzanne hung up the phone and looked at Jerry. He was smiling at her.

"Awww, that was sweet," Jerry said as he winked at Suzanne.

"I can't help it. I really was going to be nice, but I got so pissed off."

About an hour later, the phone rang. It was Marvin. "Sorry, man, I got caught up in traffic and got sick and couldn't come back. I'll be there tomorrow. Really, man, I promise."

That was it? That was his excuse? "Alright," is all Jerry could manage to say. He didn't ask any questions, he just felt it was best to leave well enough alone. All he wanted to do is get Marvin back in the house to finish the job. That was all he cared about at this point.

The next morning, Marvin showed up at nine o'clock. Jerry was counter-sinking some nails in the flooring when he arrived. He noticed that Marvin wasn't carrying any of the tools. He looked up at him without saying anything, waiting for an explanation.

"Jerry, I know you're going to hate me and never trust me again. I hate myself . . ." Marvin started sniffing and looked like he was trying to cry. His head was cocked to the side and he stared at the wall.

Jerry remained quiet. He really didn't know what to say.

Marvin continued, "Jerry, I have a bad addiction to pain killers and it has cost me everything I own. Remember when I hurt my back a few years ago? Well, I got hooked on those pills they gave me and I can't get off of them. I've sold my computer and any other stuff I could get my hands on just so I can get more medicine. Jerry, I pawned the tools yesterday. When I told you I was going home to go to the bathroom, I really went to the pawn shop to sell them again." He leaned up against the door frame for support.

"Well, let's go get the tools again. This time, they're not leaving this house. They're mine now, and you'll finish this job, understand?" Jerry said. He didn't raise his voice or put a lot of energy into getting angry.

They went to get the tools, and the flooring was installed. Another friend of Jerry's came by to help him sand and finish the floors. A natural stain was used that brought out the beauty of the oak wood grain. Jerry was proud of the way the job turned out. It was Easter, and the hardwood floors were finally done.

Chapter 13

"We can't go on like this. Are we ever going to have sex again?" Jerry said as he arranged his tools in the corner of the front room. He stood up straight and looked at Suzanne.

Suzanne was taken by surprise. She was sitting on the floor sorting nails and screws that were in a big coffee can. "Come on, don't go into this now."

"Why not? I mean, why can't I just get my rocks off?" Jerry was sweating and looked frustrated. He was still standing there looking at Suzanne.

"Well, I'm not sure why you're bringing this up right now, but I just don't want to talk about it yet." Suzanne felt uneasy discussing it. She hadn't had sexual feelings for Jerry in years. It was something she'd gotten used to, and she thought Jerry had settled for the fact that it was something that wasn't part of their relationship anymore.

"We're going to have to talk about it sometime," Jerry said as he bent down to pick up his toolbox. "I can't live this way."

"Jerry, please let's don't talk about this right now. Seriously, I just can't..."

Suzanne knew this point of contention would be the couple's undoing. The fact that she even reunited with Jerry and got into this situation weighed heavy on her heart. He had every right to ask her about sex, and she even missed it herself sometimes. But she couldn't make herself open up to him in that way anymore. Suzanne was relieved when Jerry dropped the subject, but she knew that this would be the downfall of their relationship, no matter what else they had going for them.

Up to this point, there had been no plumbing in the house. Jerry constructed a crude lean-to in the back yard, in the middle of a small thicket of trees and scrubby shrubs for Suzanne to use.

"Jerry, can you be my lookout? I've got to pee." Suzanne said as she headed out the back door. Jerry stood guard while Suzanne used the outdoor facilities. It's like camping out, thought Suzanne, only not as fun.

Since the house had finally been leveled and the floors were done, they could proceed with installing a toilet and sink in the bathroom. Suzanne had picked out an antique-looking pedestal sink and toilet. The claw foot tub had been installed, and a special order faucet was mounted. It looked old-fashioned with ceramic handles. Suzanne smiled when she looked at her lovely tub and fixture.

Jerry designed a knee wall for commode privacy and installed wainscoting halfway up the walls. Finally, they hung magnolia wallpaper and purchased a huge beveled mirror to hang above the sink. It was an awesome looking bathroom, and the first room in the house to be completed. Finally, the house was considered livable.

Jerry and Suzanne moved some of their belongings out of the apartment and into the house. Things that they didn't have an immediate use for were placed in storage. There was no sense in tripping over a bunch of stuff they didn't need while the construction process was still going on.

It was Memorial Day. Their target of being moved in by Christmas had been missed, but they were grateful to finally be in their house. As Jerry was arranging some of the furniture, the phone rang.

"Hey, Suzanne, this is Elizabeth Edwin. I know you probably don't remember me, but we met at the neighborhood meeting a few weeks ago." Suzanne thought back to the meeting and vaguely remembered talking to a woman named Elizabeth.

"Yes, I do. How are you?"

"I'm fine. I hope I'm not bothering you. Listen, you said you might want a small dog to keep in the house. I have a rat terrier that needs a home. She wants to eat my little shih-tzu," Elizabeth said before Suzanne could get a word in.

Suzanne didn't recall saying she actually wanted a dog. She remembered a conversation about dogs in general. "Well, we just moved into the house we're renovating." Suzanne looked around herself at her belongings mixed in with construction tools, wood leaning against the wall, and rolls of insulation stacked in the corner of the room. "It's awful dirty around here. We're kind of roughing it right now. I just don't know."

"Are you sure? She's so cute. She'd make a good little pet for you."

"Uh, well, I'll have to check with my husband. And it might be awhile before we'd be able to take her. Could you wait a few weeks?"

"Well, not really. I've got to go ahead and do something with her. She's going to drive Freckles crazy. If you don't want the dog, that's okay. My dad says he'll take her if I can't find anybody else," answered Elizabeth.

"Can you hold on a minute?" Suzanne covered the receiver with her hand. "Jerry, what do you think about getting a dog?"

"Huh? I don't think we need to be getting a dog, of all things."

"Can we at least go look at her?"

Jerry hesitated and answered, "I guess so. But you know we can't get a dog for a few months. It's bad timing right now." Jerry was kneeling on the floor looking at an electrical outlet.

"She says she's got to get rid of her now because she's driving her other dog crazy," Suzanne said in a pleading voice. She wrinkled her nose and waited for Jerry to reply.

"Do you want a dog that badly?" Jerry asked Suzanne.

"Well . . ." Suzanne paused. "I haven't had one in a long time, and she's a small dog that we could keep in the house. Can we at least go look at her, please?" She asked expectantly.

"Yeah, we can go look at it. But if you decide you want it, we have to watch it all the time, because of all this mess around here," Jerry answered as he dusted off his knees from being on the floor. "It'll be eating the insulation."

"Ha ha," Suzanne said to Jerry. "By the way, she's a she, not an 'it.'" She stuck her tongue out at Jerry.

"Elizabeth, we can come over to look at her. When's a good time?"

Suzanne and Jerry walked two blocks to Elizabeth's house the following evening to see the dog. When Elizabeth came to the door, they heard a sharp bark in the background and looked at each other. Maybe this wasn't a good idea after all.

"Just come on in here and see this girl," Elizabeth said as she opened the door.

The little dog came bounding toward them as they stepped inside. Suzanne squatted down and rubbed the dog's soft ears. She thought it was one of the cutest puppies she'd ever seen.

Jerry carried the dog home. She wasn't house-trained. This was evident when the puppy squatted to pee in the house as soon as he sat her down in the entry way inside the front door.

Nevertheless, she immediately had the run of the house. This actually pleased Suzanne. She now had something to focus on besides her own unhappiness. She felt good as she watched the puppy frolic throughout the rooms. The little dog was so clean and sleek that she looked out of place in the midst of all the dust and debris lying around.

Jerry and Suzanne had set up temporary living quarters in one of the rooms of the house. Suzanne placed a folded blanket in the corner so the dog could sleep in the same room with them. The puppy took to her new bed right away, keeping her toys protectively on the blanket next to her.

"What are we going to name her?" Suzanne asked Jerry.

"What about Butterbean?" he said as he patted the dog on the head.

"No, I don't think so!" Suzanne said laughing. "Why Butterbean?"

"Your mama used to talk about somebody named Butterbean. Remember that? I just think it would be funny."

Suzanne thought about it for a minute and remembered her mother calling somebody that nickname. She smiled at the thought of what her mother's reaction would be to naming the dog Butterbean. "Well, unless we think of something better, I think that's a good name for her."

Suzanne enjoyed playing with her new pet. She bathed the fragile little dog and brushed her fur. There was even a doggy sweater she saw at the pet store that she couldn't resist.

Suzanne was glad to have something to love; at times she felt alone. Co-workers and friends was what she and Jerry had become, Suzanne sadly realized. She wasn't prepared to tackle the issue of their crumbling marriage at this point. She prayed at night and hoped that the lack of communication between her and Jerry wouldn't halt the progress of the house. They had come so far already; if either of them were to get out of this situation with their sanity and without going bankrupt, they had to finish what they started together.

On the third morning after the move to the house, Suzanne was startled to see Jerry suddenly sit up in bed. It wasn't yet light outside. "It's the police," said Jerry.

"What?" Suzanne sat up in bed and could see blue lights flashing out front. She squinted as she looked at the clock. It was five o'clock in the morning. She scrambled out of bed and hurriedly put on her jeans. "I wonder what's going on. Can you see anything?"

Jerry opened the blinds enough to look outside. "Gladys is out there talking to a policeman. They're walking toward our house."

Jerry grabbed a shirt and the pants he had taken off the night before that were lying in the floor and hurried out the front door. Suzanne followed closely behind.

"What's going on, officer?" Jerry asked as he took long strides across the yard.

"That's him. He's the one who tore up my yard and he's killing my tree. He's flooding my basement and he put his old dirt in my yard," said Gladys in a loud, accusing voice as she pointed at Jerry. She was wearing an old housecoat and had pants on underneath it. "They're trying to run me off, but I ain't going nowhere!" She directed her last comment to Jerry.

"Oh, brother," Jerry said below his breath. "Officer, she's driving us nuts with this stuff. We haven't done a thing to her, but she keeps accusing us of stealing from her and, well, all that other stuff she just said to you."

The officer listened to Jerry, nodding. "I understand." He turned to Gladys and said in a monotone voice, "Ma'am, this is a matter for civil court. I can't tell what damage has been done. You'd have to get a lawyer for this."

The police officer didn't pretend to care. He turned to walk back to his car, saying something into the radio he had on his shoulder.

Jerry and Suzanne followed the officer back to his car to discuss the situation. "She's absolutely insane. I can't believe she'd call the police on us. I have never in my life had to put up with something this stupid!" said Suzanne. She was half awake and her voice was hoarse. "Really, we just don't even know how to handle this lunatic anymore." Suzanne felt overwhelmed by the fact that she was actually describing her situation to a police officer.

"Y'all better quit lying about me," Gladys yelled from her porch. She was pointing at the three talking on the street next to the police car. She paced back and forth watching them. Her eyes narrowed with suspicion. "They're tryin' to run me off, but I've been here twenty years and I ain't goin' nowhere!" she shrieked. The neighbors across the street turned on their front porch lights and looked out of their window.

The officer watched Gladys' show with no particular expression on his face. "Oh, I know she's not playing with a full deck. We've had to come out here several times to calm her down over the years. I know it's easy for me to say, but just try to get along with her the best you can and call us if you have any more problems. Unless she does something to you or your property, it's really out of our hands." He gave a sympathetic smile as he turned to get into his car.

Jerry and Suzanne went back into the house purposely trying not to look next door. Out of the corner of her eye, Suzanne could see Gladys staring ominously at her from her porch.

"What are we going to do about this?" Suzanne asked, as she got dressed for work. "I can't take all this friction. Why can't she just leave us alone?" She sat on the bed and looked at her shoes on the floor.

"I don't know. At least the police know about some of her past problems. You heard him say that they've been out here before with her acting up," Jerry answered. He'd put on a flannel shirt over his t-shirt and was tying his work boots. "I'll tell you this much, I'm not doing anything else for them again. No more rides to the store, no more picking up prescriptions, no more fixing things. They're on their own."

"Uh, Jerry, I don't think Gladys or her son is going to ask you to take them anywhere any more." Suzanne smiled. "At least that's one blessing out of this big feud she's started."

Suzanne finished getting ready to go to work. She decided to pack some dirty laundry into her truck. She planned to take a couple of loads to the laundromat during her lunch break at work. After digging in the dirt and all the other grimy projects they had to do, there was never a shortage of dirty clothes.

The days were long, and there was no time spent on any kind of personal pursuits or interests other than working on house projects. When the couple wasn't working on the house, they were working on things related to the house, or working to make money. The monotony of it all was wearing them down.

Suzanne was so exhausted and frustrated by everything that was going on, that she often cried when no one was around. Butterbean offered a little comfort. Her brown eyes looked sad when she watched Suzanne cry. She snuggled into Suzanne's arms at night offering warmth and occasional protective growls at noises she heard outside.

The next Saturday, Suzanne's father Paul pulled up to the curb in front of the house. As he stepped up the walkway, he had a bad feeling as he glanced toward Gladys' house. She was sitting on the porch rocking back and forth. Paul waved hello to her as he walked past. She didn't acknowledge him; she looked straight ahead and continued rocking.

Jerry, Paul and Gilbert had already made plans to go to the hardware store for supplies. As they left the house, Paul noticed that Gladys wasn't on the porch anymore, and he was relieved that he didn't have to walk past her again.

Suzanne decided to work on some drywall in the house while the guys were gone. She was mudding and taping the area that would soon be the dining room. The windows were open, and the cool spring air felt good to her as she worked on perfecting her drywall skills.

About an hour later, Suzanne heard a car door slam, so she looked out the front window to see if Jerry had returned. Instead, she saw Gladys walking up the steps of her house. Immediately, Suzanne felt defensive when she looked at the big woman's bulky frame tramping up the walkway. She tried to disregard her feelings. She resented the fact that she was allowing another person to dictate the way she felt.

A dirty looking, heavy-set man was right behind Gladys carrying groceries. There was another big man, equally as grubby looking, carrying a bag of groceries as well. Suzanne paused with her work for a moment to watch the odd parade.

Gladys stopped right before she reached her front door and spoke to the man behind her. "See what they're doing to me? Look, they're tearing up my yard. See that?" She pointed her chubby finger at the ground between the houses. Her big bosom was heaving with every heavy breath.

With the windows wide open, Suzanne could hear everything that was being said as if the conversation was going on in the same room. She quickly stood to the side of the window so that she couldn't be seen; looking around the edge just enough to observe what was going on. She watched Gladys' gestures become more animated as she continued to complain.

One of the men walked between the houses and said, "I don't remember what your yard looked like before." He was looking up and down the walkway between the houses. "I can't really tell. What did you say is wrong with it?" He was scratching the back of his neck. He looked a little bothered by Gladys' insistence on him looking at everything to which she pointed.

"Woof" Butterbean barked. She was trying to sleep in a spot of sunshine coming in through the window when she heard voices outside.

"Shush!" Suzanne whispered to the dog. She listened intently to what was being said outside.

"They're trying to run me out of here. They call me names and Jerry pushed me into this door right here, see?" Gladys' pouty voice trailed off.

Oh, my gosh, she's lying about us! Susanne thought. She couldn't see Gladys anymore from the angle where she stood. She tried to move a little to see what was going on. She imagined Gladys pointing at the door, showing those big guys where Jerry had supposedly pushed her into it.

The other man, who had rested against a post after setting the bag of groceries on the porch, spoke up. "Listen, Gladys, if they're bothering you, I can do something about that. I ain't going to sit around while somebody's messing with my sister." He was sweating, and he looked unstable on his feet as if he had been drinking. His balance was thrown off when his hand slipped off the post he was leaning against.

"Yeah, they're bothering me alright. They're trying to run me out of here. They think they can come in here and tell me what to do."

"You want me to go over there and talk some sense into them?" The man pulled up his pants and looked hard at Suzanne's house. "We can take care of this right now."

Suzanne's heart was pounding. She felt like she had to diffuse this situation before the guys got back from the hardware store. What if they pulled up and these two guys jumped on them?

Suzanne felt sick and her mouth went dry. Should she stay put and pray that these two guys would leave without causing any trouble, or should she say something? Surely they wouldn't hurt her; she was a woman. She struggled with the decision for a moment before she decided to confront this situation.

She looked out the window again and saw that Gladys had moved to where she could see her. Gladys had her hands on her hips, and was looking at the man who was talking.

With the drywall knife still in her hand, Suzanne went out onto the front porch. She didn't know if she was making things worse by speaking up, but she felt like she had to say something. To her amazement, she remained calm as she faced her neighbor. She even managed to smile a little.

"You get back in that house, you slut! Whore! You fucking bitch!" Gladys was shouting loudly. She had tears in her eyes and she was swinging her arms wildly. "You trashy slut!"

Suzanne was stunned by Gladys' obscene language. This was the most explosive reaction she had ever demonstrated. Sweat was streaming down the sides of her face, and she looked like she was going to blow up. She was so out of control that the man who had threatened to take care of the situation for her was trying to calm her down as he grabbed at her swinging arms. Suzanne thought Gladys might hit the man as he tried to restrain her. It was a clumsy display, especially since the man could barely stand upright on his own without falling over.

"Get in the house, Gladys! Stop hollering at her." He pushed her into the house and followed her inside.

Suzanne could hear him scolding Gladys. "You've got to stop cussing and hollering at that girl. She's going to call the police and what do you think is going to happen? Woman, the police don't like me no how."

"I hate them people! They ain't done nothing but mistreat me since they've been here. Them mother-fuckers ain't going to run me out of my own house!" Gladys screamed. Suzanne could hear scuffling and things falling as the man tried to get control of Gladys. She was crying hysterically.

Suzanne was still standing on her porch feeling completely unnerved. The other man had sat on Gladys' porch step and was looking back and forth from the street to Gladys' front door. He didn't look at Suzanne until she spoke.

"I guess I better start out by saying that we've never done anything to hurt anybody. If we messed up her yard, we'll fix it. We've tried so hard to be good neighbors."

The man was quiet and only looked at Suzanne for a few seconds at a time. He acted like he was intimidated by the fact that she'd come out to talk to him.

"I've gone and gotten prescriptions for her and taken her to the grocery store. My husband has taken her to the liquor store to cash her disability check." Suzanne paused and waited for some reaction from the man. He only nodded.

"We've been nice to her, but she's not being nice to us. What little dirt we've moved around in our yard couldn't have possibly done the kind of damage she's talking about. She says her basement is flooded, and she says we're stealing her water. Well, maybe her plumbing is leaking. That would flood her basement and it would make her water bill go up. Maybe she needs a plumber to look at what's going on in her basement."

The man shook his head. "Well, that's my sister, and she don't lie. I don't know what to do about all of this. She's pretty upset." He looked like he wanted to be somewhere else.

Gladys was rampaging through her house. All of her windows were open and Suzanne could hear things crashing as Gladys stomped. She came out on the porch and yelled at her brother, "What are you doing talking to that bitch out here? Don't be talking to that trashy slut!" She then slammed the door as she stormed back into her house. She was like a beast raging out of control. The house literally looked like it was shaking.

"Well, if you ever want to talk about it, we're here," Suzanne said. She walked into the house, locked the door behind herself and sat on the floor. She took several deep breaths trying to calm her pounding heartbeat. "God, please help us get through this. Please . . ."

Suzanne could still hear Gladys spewing insults and vulgar language. "I wish them people would die!" Gladys screamed. She was crying uncontrollably. "If them people know what's good for them, they'll get the hell out of my neighborhood!"

Some Christian, Suzanne thought as she hugged her knees to her chest. She sat like that on the floor for several minutes. She then stood up to watch for the Jerry, Paul and Gilbert. Surely they'd be back soon.

Within a few minutes that seemed like an eternity, Jerry pulled his truck in front of the house and got out to unload it. He looked up toward the house and saw Suzanne standing in the doorway shaking her head, eyes wide with an upset look on her face.

Paul and Gilbert began unloading the truck while Jerry went up to the house to check on Suzanne. "What's wrong?"

"Jerry, she's been on a tirade since you left. She's been cussing me out and calling me names. She's really acting like a nut case. I've never seen anybody act like that before," Suzanne said shaking.

"Well, try to calm down. It's all over now." He patted her on the shoulder like a good friend.

"Are those men still out there? She had her two brothers with her. They were carrying her groceries, then when they got up to the porch, all hell broke loose."

"No, I didn't see any guys at her house. And she's not out there on her porch right now either. Let me help your daddy get some of that stuff out of the truck and I'll be right back in. Then I want you to tell me all about it," he said as he headed back out the door.

Suzanne stayed just inside the doorway so she couldn't be seen. Next door, she heard the screen door slam and she knew

Gladys had come back out on her porch. She felt her stomach tighten.

"I'm going to sue you, Jerry, for messing up my yard and flooding my basement. And stealing my water!" Gladys yelled at Jerry.

"Gladys, please. Just drop it. Nobody's stealing anything from you, and I'm getting tired of hearing the same crap from you day after day. Please just leave us alone and let us get some work done." Jerry faced her as he spoke.

"You better keep your nasty ass wife in the house and she better not never talk to me again if she knows what's good for her," Gladys screamed as she pointed her finger toward Jerry's house. She seemed infuriated that Jerry would dismiss her threats.

Jerry ignored her as he walked to the truck to bring some supplies into the house.

"Don't you act like you can't hear me. I mean it. That little bitch better keep her fucking mouth closed. Trying to talk to my brothers about me -- telling lies!"

Jerry stopped in the middle of the yard, his arms holding two-by-fours, and looked at Gladys with such disgust that she shrank in his gaze. "Don't you ever talk to my wife like that again, do you hear me? I don't want to EVER hear you insult her like that again."

Gladys took a step backward as she realized that someone was actually standing up to her. "You tell her to mind her own business then, Jerry!" she yelled. She stormed back into her house slamming the door.

No wonder her door looks like it's about to fall off its hinges, Suzanne thought. She decided not to say anything to Jerry as he finished unloading the truck. Feeling a strong sense of despair, she went inside and started working on the drywall again.

The next day was Sunday. Suzanne said to Jerry, "Let's go ahead and flatten out the dirt on the side of the house between us and Gladys. That's one thing she's upset about, you know. Even though you and I know it's not causing her any problems, maybe it'll generate some good will. What do you think?"

"You're kidding, right?" Jerry said smiling.

Suzanne shook her head. "Please, let's just do this, okay? I can't stand this fighting anymore."

He shook his head and turned away from Suzanne. "We're going to be working out there again in a couple of weeks, and we'll just have to smooth out that dirt all over again. It's cosmetic, for God's sake, and nobody can even see it from the road. Here we go, letting her dictate our lives."

Suzanne's head hurt as she tried to reason with him. "If we could just work on it for a couple of hours, it might help. Come on, Jerry. You make all the decisions about everything around here. You direct me from the time we get up till the time we go to bed. Can't I make a suggestion now and then?"

"Oh, hell. I guess so. Let me go get some yard tools from the basement. This is a fucked up situation, you know that?"

They went out to the side of the house to begin the dreaded chore of raking and manipulating dirt. Jerry carried two rakes, a wheelbarrow, and a shovel to the side of the house next to Gladys' house. Suzanne followed behind with work gloves and grass seed in a bucket. Her stomach was in knots, she knew this wouldn't be pleasant. The side yard actually looked level with the exception of the ground being lumpy right next to their house. Suzanne couldn't understand why Gladys was even upset about it.

They proceeded to rake the dirt flat. After working for about fifteen minutes, Suzanne heard the screen door open and slam shut next door. She didn't look up, but she could feel Gladys looking at her. She silently prayed for enough strength to get through this situation. After all, this was just an old woman who was mentally ill. Surely this was something she could handle.

Gladys had come out with a ball of yarn and sat down with an afghan she had apparently just started knitting. "Don't you put your dirt in my yard," she said as she sat there clicking her knitting needles. She didn't even look up when she said it. Her voice sounded like fingernails on a chalkboard to Suzanne.

Suzanne saw Jerry stop raking and look up. She motioned for him to be quiet. He reluctantly bit his lip and didn't say anything as he resumed his work.

"I said, don't you put none of your dirt in my yard." Gladys' tone was low and threatening. "I'm telling you for the last time."

Jerry opened his mouth to speak, but Suzanne stopped him. "Let me handle this."

Suzanne walked over to face Gladys while she spoke to her. "Gladys, we'd like to fix your yard today," Suzanne started to explain. She was having a hard time keeping her voice even, but with a potentially explosive situation, she had to stay unruffled. She even tried to look friendly and smile. It was a hard stretch given the fact that Gladys had called her a whore and a slut. "You've been complaining for a while now about this dirt. I don't know how else to make you happy except to try to fix it the way you want it."

"I don't want you in my yard. I'm going to sue you for property damage. I've done talked to a lawyer, and he told me I could sue you for flooding my basement and for trying to kill my tree." Gladys twisted her head to face Suzanne.

Suzanne was closer to Gladys than she'd ever been, and she could see the hate in her eyes. Gladys' voice was thick with medication, and her teeth were filthy. Suzanne wondered if she ever brushed them.

"Please let us fix your yard. I'm asking your permission. Wouldn't you like to have nice green grass here to walk on?

We could fix it up beautiful if you'll let us." Suzanne felt like she was begging, which sickened her, but she stood fast and tried to stay fixed on her goal to get this done. She didn't know that Jerry was standing behind her looking at Gladys with malice, daring her with his eyes to say one wrong thing.

Gladys sat quietly for a moment, not looking at Suzanne. Instead she looked like she was thinking about some far off thing. She straightened her shoulders, acting very superior as she spoke, "I guess so." She trailed off at the end of her answer and started working on her knitting again. She acted triumphant and majestic, as if she were giving her royal subjects permission to please her. Suzanne wanted to reach out and slap her face for acting like an ass, but she maintained her composure.

Suzanne realized that she was mentally and physically worn-out from the confrontation with the woman. Her adrenaline level had gotten so high that she was shaking as she tried to work her aggression out by chopping at the dirt.

A neighbor whom Suzanne hadn't seen before was walking down the street and came onto Gladys' porch to visit with her. Their voices were loud enough to hear, though Suzanne wasn't the least bit interested in listening. "Who-wee, it's turned hot today, ain't it?" he asked Gladys as he slunk into the chair next to her. His t-shirt had sweat stains all over it.

"Yeah," she said flatly.

He casually looked at Jerry and Suzanne working. Then he drew his attention back to his conversation with Gladys. "Yeah, yeah, it sure is hot! What kind of tree is that in your yard, Miss Gladys?"

"Cottonwood," she muttered.

"Cottonwood? I don't know about no cottonwood trees," he said, trying to make conversation.

"It rains down white cotton in the summer. Come back around here in a few weeks and you'll see." She got up and went into her house, slamming the door behind herself, leaving her visitor alone on the front porch. He lifted his hat to scratch his head and sat there for a little while longer before nonchalantly wandering down the street.

Jerry and Suzanne looked at each other and rolled their eyes. Suzanne acted like she was gagging herself and Jerry smirked back at her. All the hard work they had to do, and on top of it all, they had to baby sit a crazy neighbor.

When they completed the leveling and seeding of the area, Jerry and Suzanne decided to get something to eat. They went inside and cleaned up to leave. As they were getting into Jerry's truck, they saw that Gladys had walked across the street and was talking to some neighbors. She was clapping her hands and grinning. She waved at Jerry and Suzanne. "Whatever," Suzanne said to Jerry. "I don't care as long as we're not fighting. I hate hearing her voice. She sounds like a fucking magpie."

When they got home from picking up lunch, they decided to sit on their front porch for a change and enjoy the spring weather. Butterbean was tethered to her dog run in the front yard.

A few minutes later, Gladys walked down the sidewalk in front of their house. She had on a big housecoat and slippers, though it was well into the middle of the day. When she passed Butterbean, the little dog began to bark at her. Gladys seemed totally oblivious to Jerry and Suzanne's presence on their front porch as she stood in front of Butterbean. She stared at the dog as if she was in some type of stupor. Then she stepped forward just enough to make the dog think she was going to come near it. The dog strained at the tether, barking at the woman, becoming aggravated because it couldn't reach her on the sidewalk.

"She's teasing that dog," Suzanne said quietly to Jerry. "Watch."

Gladys stepped back and forth in front of the dog, testing to see how far it could go, staying just out of its reach. Butterbean barked and yelped with frustration.

Gladys leered at the dog as it twisted and jumped, trying to get to her. "Damn dog!" she said as she turned to walk down the sidewalk to her house.

"I swear, she's got no sense at all, does she?" Suzanne said to Jerry as Gladys walked away.

"I'd say not," Jerry said as he chewed his sandwich.

Chapter 14

The next few weeks were spent working hard as ever on the house. It was now July, and work on various projects seemed to go quicker and easier with the nice summer weather.

The kitchen was finally taking shape. The cabinets had been hung in the kitchen and the drywall was finally ready to be taped and mudded. Jerry discovered that the backside of the brick fireplace that extended into the kitchen had been covered with plaster. He thought it would look nice to have the contrast of brick and drywall in the kitchen. He knocked the plaster off the bricks with a small sledgehammer, careful to avoid chipping the brick. He then washed it down with an acid wash to clean off any excess plaster. This was a messy process that had an atrocious smell. The newly-exposed brick and mortar were then sealed with a masonry sealer.

The kitchen turned out to be quite large since not only was the existing kitchen space utilized, but the old dilapidated back porch and pantry had also been incorporated into the room. Even though it was still a dusty construction site, Suzanne was relieved to see the beginnings of a real kitchen.

The part of the kitchen that used to be the broken down back porch had a large screen window that Jerry replaced with a custom-made, double-pane window. It allowed lots of beautiful, natural light into the room. Suzanne loved to stand in the warm morning rays of the sun that came through the window.

Once the drywall was completed, Suzanne painted the kitchen cabinets a pale green and sponge painted the walls with a similar color. It looked cheerful and became Suzanne's favorite room. The sink was hooked up, which was a glorious sight. Finally, no more washing dishes in the bathtub!

As Jerry and Suzanne arrived home from taking Butterbean for a walk, Suzanne followed Jerry's gaze toward the roof of the house. He had a concerned look on his face. "Hmm," he said thoughtfully.

"What are you looking at?"

"You see that huge limb up there hanging over the house?"

Suzanne's eyes followed the limb to its source. It was connected to the big cottonwood tree in Gladys' yard. "What about it?"

"If that thing falls on the house, you know it's going to do some major damage. I've been watching it since we bought the place."

"Well, you never said anything. I never really paid that much attention to it, but you're right. That's a big sucker alright. I'd hate to be under it when it falls."

"We'll be under it when it falls. Don't you see? It would fall on the roof right over where we sleep."

Suzanne hated the thought of their house being damaged by the limb, but she also knew that they'd have to talk to Gladys if they really wanted to do anything about it. Since tensions with her had subsided somewhat, maybe they could approach the subject and discuss it with her. Suzanne envisioned going over to talk to Gladys and her reaction being one of cooperation. Suzanne laughed at her own naiveté.

Jerry saw Gladys sitting on her porch one afternoon as he drove up to the front of his house. He watched her for a few minutes to see if she was in a good mood. Fuck it. I'm going to go ahead and talk to her, he thought.

"Hey, Gladys, how's it going today?" He approached slowly. He wondered if she'd speak back to him or dismiss him like an insignificant fly buzzing around her face.

Gladys looked at Jerry as if she were merely tolerating him. "Alright."

"I wanted to talk to you about that limb up there that's hanging over our house."

Gladys squinted as she looked up toward Jerry's roofline.

"It's hanging right over our house. See? It's a dead limb. You can tell because it doesn't have any leaves on it and the bark is falling off." He pointed at the tree as he talked in a friendly, casual tone.

"What about it?"

"If it falls on our house, it's going to really tear up our roof," Jerry explained. He sounded like he was talking to a child. "We were thinking, if we pay for half and you pay for half, we could get it cut. I already checked on a price. It would be about a hundred dollars. If you could pay fifty dollars, we'd also pay fifty. Do you want to do that? Does that sound fair to you?"

"Yeah, I guess I could." Gladys looked at Jerry with a suspicious expression, but she sounded agreeable.

"Believe me, you won't be sorry. If that thing fell on our roof, you'd have to pay for the roof to be repaired, and that could be a lot of money."

Gladys immediately had a look of anger wash over her face. She remained silent for a moment and looked ahead at the street. "Yeah," she finally answered in an expressionless voice which contradicted her frown.

Jerry hesitated as he saw her disposition change almost the instant his words left his mouth. He thought about talking to her more, but decided he'd leave well enough alone. He felt like he had said too much already. "Okay. We'll talk to you later!" he said as he turned to walk back to his house.

"I hate that you even had to bring that up," said Suzanne when Jerry came back into the house from talking to Gladys. "I was watching you talk to her out the window. I think you did a good job."

"Thanks. Seriously, if that thing falls, we're going to be minus one roof," Jerry answered. "It looks like she's trying to come around and be nice. I think I just took her by surprise, that's all. Let's give her a chance."

Jerry woke abruptly the next morning to a knock on the front door. He sat up and listened. Suzanne woke up and looked at the clock. It was 4:50 a.m. Jerry got out of bed, walked to the front door, and pulled the curtain back slightly to look out onto the front porch.

"Gladys," Jerry said.

"What's she doing here?" Suzanne scrambled to pull on some sweatpants as she moved toward the front door with Jerry. She stood behind him as he opened the door just enough to talk to Gladys.

"What is it?" Jerry asked, trying not to sound too annoyed, but not quite taking the edge off his voice.

"I decided I don't want you to cut my tree. I've been thinking about it all night, and I can't let you touch it." Gladys looked arrogant as she spoke with an air of self-importance.

"Do we have to talk about this now? It's five o'clock in the morning. Go home, Gladys. We can talk about it later." Jerry closed the door, but Gladys was still standing there, looking into the front door window.

"You're going to kill my tree. I ain't got no fifty dollars to give you. My light bill came in, and my boy ain't working. I can't afford no fifty dollars to give you." She kept talking as if the door was still open, her raspy, whiny voice sounded like she was standing right there in the living room.

Jerry opened the door again and said, "We'll talk about this some other time." Gladys started walking away from the door, down the front porch steps, and Jerry added, "And don't come back here at this time of morning again to tell me something stupid like that."

Gladys kept walking down the walkway to the sidewalk and toward her house.

The next day at work, Suzanne called and spoke to an attorney about their rights. "If her limb is hanging over your house, you have the right to cut it without asking. You own your property and infinitely what's above it and below it," the attorney explained.

"Yeah, I understand that, but as soon as we cut it, it's going to be a really nasty situation. She'll throw a fit and act like she's having a heart attack or something," Suzanne told the attorney.

"Well, when that limb falls, the insurance company is going to find someone liable. If you know the limb is hanging over your house and you don't get it cut, they could find you liable. The only way to get the ball out of your court is to send your neighbor a certified letter telling her that she has a limb over your property and that there's an eminent danger of the limb falling on your house causing considerable damage. In the letter, be sure to mention that you've asked her to remove the limb numerous times and that her attitude has been one of no cooperation. Also, be sure to mention that if the limb falls on your house, she'll be financially liable," advised the attorney.

After Suzanne got off the phone, she composed the letter just as the attorney had recommended, being sure to mention the issues and using the phrases he suggested. After work, she stopped by the post office and sent the letter to Gladys by certified mail. Suzanne knew she was about to start another war.

Two days later, Suzanne parked in front of her house after work and stopped to get the mail before going into her house. In the mailbox was the certified proof of mailing card with

Gladys' signature. Also in the box, laying on top of the other mail, was the letter that Suzanne had sent Gladys. It wasn't in the envelope; it was folded up on top of the rest of the mail.

Suzanne looked up to see Gladys staring at her from her front porch. Suzanne smiled to herself and started walking toward her front steps. From next door Gladys yelled at her, "You're playing secretary writing me letters. Let me tell you, I was a secretary one time, and I was a better secretary than you!" Suzanne stopped to look at Gladys showing no emotion, just boldly looking back at Gladys to show that she wasn't going to be intimidated anymore.

Gladys was sitting on her green chaise lounge facing Suzanne with her legs wide open. She wore red pants and a green sweater with fuzzy house shoes on her feet. "I ain't cutting that limb and I don't care if it falls on your house and knocks it down. You hear me? Besides, I've been in this house twenty years and that limb ain't going to fall. I don't know who you think you are, you heifer, but you ain't getting nothing over on me!"

This was better than a cartoon, Suzanne thought. She resumed walking up her steps without answering Gladys. She was protected now in case it did fall, and she had the signed certified letter card to prove it. Nothing further needed to be said.

On Sunday, a fancy black car pulled up in front of Gladys' house and she got out with a big man in a purple suit. She was walking up the sidewalk toward her front steps when she noticed Jerry and Suzanne planting flowers in their front yard.

"That's them. They're the ones who want to cut my tree down!" She was pointing her cane at Jerry and Suzanne. "They think they own my house. They're trying to run me off." She was walking slowly up the steps, shouting loudly as she went.

"Why is she bringing this crap up to that guy?" Suzanne whispered to Jerry.

Jerry didn't answer Suzanne; instead he stood and looked directly at the man with Gladys, who appeared to be a minister as he was carrying a Bible and a briefcase, and said, "That's not true. See that limb up there? If it falls on our house, she's financially liable for it. We're just trying to keep her from being out a lot of money. We offered to help pay to have it cut, but she's been so ugly to us, she can pay for it herself."

The gentleman in the purple suit thought about what Jerry said and nodded in agreement as he stood looking up at the limb. "Miss Gladys, they ain't trying to cut your tree down. Look here, they're just trying to help you."

No sooner had the words left his mouth than Gladys took off toward her house running, her fat body jiggling in all directions. Suzanne looked at Jerry and stifled a laugh. It was funny to see this woman, who pretended to be feeble and sick all the time, run up the steps to her porch and slam the door. She looked like a kid having a tantrum.

The minister followed her up her steps. "Miss Gladys, you come on out here now, you hear? Ain't nobody trying to hurt you out here! Miss Gladys?" He pleaded as he kept knocking on her door with rapid knocks.

Gladys swung the door open with so much force that it ricocheted against the house almost hitting her on the rebound. She was crying loud with tears streaming down her face. She hollered, "They're trying to cut my tree down and they did property damage to my house. I'm going to sue them. I've been here for twenty years, and Lord knows I ain't never had no problems with nobody like I do them. They want me to move out so they can have my house, that's what they're wanting to do. They're evil!" The last word, "evil", came out as a scream in the minister's face.

The minister put his hand out to touch Gladys' arm to console her. "Miss Gladys, come on now, calm down. Don't be this way," he begged.

Gladys jerked her arm away from him and yelled in his face, "You get out of here and don't you never come back!" She ran inside and slammed the door. Jerry and Suzanne could hear her screaming inside her house.

The minister paused for a minute looking disappointed. Then he took his Bible and briefcase and got in his car to leave. He looked back at Jerry as he pulled away. He waved at Jerry with a forced smile. Jerry waved back.

Chapter 15

The next Saturday morning, Jerry decided to get up early to work on the electrical wiring. He was close to being finished and was glad that he wouldn't have to keep going back and forth between the outlets, switches and breaker box. He had carefully labeled the breakers as he went along and tested the results of his sometimes ambiguous instructions from his do-it-yourself books. He admired his own ingenuity since this was the first time he'd ever taken on such a complex task.

Jerry had asked Suzanne to do her daily chore of picking up tools, cleaning what she could, and organizing the house. He knew that she was tired of rearranging their clutter all the time, but he was resolute about getting the wiring completed, and he didn't want her to get into a project that she couldn't easily drop when he called for her to help him run wires through walls.

Outside the sun was shining. Jerry looked forward to a productive day. He watched out the back door as Suzanne tied Butterbean to a shade tree. He started whistling to himself as he cut a piece of black electrical tape to join a couple of wires. His knees were already beginning to hurt as he knelt on them to do his work.

Within an hour, Jerry heard Gladys singing. "Here we go again," Jerry said aloud though no one was around to hear him. He crawled on his hands and knees to look out the window. He could see Gladys doing her familiar pacing across her porch, shaking her fist at the sky as she sang. Jerry went back to the outlet he was working on and tried to concentrate on what he was doing. He started feeling hot and frustrated. Gladys' incessant wailing had reached a raucous volume, and she showed no signs of letting up. He laid down his screwdriver and took a deep breath. "Why am I letting this get to me?" he asked himself as he tried to conjure up a peaceful scene in his mind. He realized he hadn't gone fishing in almost a year.

"Suzanne! Hey, where are you?" Jerry yelled as he got up off the floor and dusted off his jeans.

"I'm up here putting some stuff away. What do you want?" Suzanne sounded annoyed.

"Are you hungry? Let's go get something to eat. Her singing is driving me crazy, and I've just got to get out of here for awhile. Maybe while we're gone, she'll shut the hell up."

Suzanne walked down the stairs looking a little relieved, "Actually, yes, I could use a bite to eat. If she realizes that we've left, she might hush for a while. Most of the time, I think she does it because she knows it bugs us."

"Oh, I know she does."

"I wish I could do what my mother would tell me to do if she were here. She'd say just ignore it."

"Yeah, right."

They walked out of the house to get into the truck, paying no attention to Gladys sitting next door still singing on her porch. They held hands walking down the sidewalk and smiled at each other as they walked. Suzanne couldn't help but glance at Gladys as she got into the truck. Suzanne did a double-take when she saw how Gladys was sitting. She was lying upside-down on her green chaise lounge with her feet sticking up in the air. Her hair looked like it had been slicked back with some type of gel or hairspray.

Suzanne whispered, "Look, Jerry, look!"

Jerry looked over at Gladys and turned back around so she wouldn't see him laughing. "Hmmm, that looks comfortable," he managed to say.

Gladys' wardrobe didn't disappoint today. She was wearing red knit pants and a plaid shawl draped across her shoulders. She was bare-footed.

After they got finished eating, Jerry and Suzanne went back to their house and parked in front of it.

"Well, she's still out there." Suzanne could feel her resentment turning into anger.

"At least she's sitting upright now," Jerry mused as he took the keys out of the ignition.

Gladys was smoking a cigarette and had a large glass of what looked like iced tea. When she saw her neighbors park out front, she smashed the cigarette butt into her ash tray and started singing again. She gave a nasty look at Jerry as he got out of the truck and started practically screaming whatever gospel song she was singing. Jerry looked at the steps as he calmly walked toward his house, purposely avoiding Gladys' stare.

"Mother-fucker," Gladys hissed at Jerry as he got closer to her.

It seemed that something snapped in Jerry and there was no ignoring this abuse any longer. Suzanne watched him stop abruptly and look up at Gladys.

"Would you please be a little quieter? You've been singing all morning, and we really would like to get a little peace around here today, if that's possible," Jerry began. He was talking in a controlled, polite tone of voice.

"You go to hell!" Gladys screamed. "I can't help it if you don't like gospel music!" She started singing along with her radio and smacked her leg with her hand. She then raised her arms in the air and praised the Lord.

"It doesn't matter what you're singing, you're too loud," Jerry said with a raised voice. He put his hands on his hips and looked like he wanted to go over and put them around the old woman's neck.

Gladys stopped singing and glared at Jerry furiously. "Jerry, you ain't going to run me off. This is my house and I ain't going nowhere. I'm going to sing as loud as I want to every day. The Lord sees you, and he's going to get you for what you're doing to me. I'll make sure he gets you like I made sure he got my husband!"

Jerry started to answer her, but she interrupted with more shouting, "You're a fucking bastard, Jerry. You think you can tell me what to do, but you can't. You're going to find out!" She spat the words at him. "Just who in the hell do you think you are, trying to come in here and fix up some old house."

One of the neighbors from across the street stepped out on his porch to see what was going on. A child riding his bike down the street stopped and stared. Gladys was oblivious to the scene she was making.

"Look how you talk to us. The names you call us, the cussing. How many times do you think we're going to just walk away? Are we supposed to just take this off of you?" Jerry said, his voice getting thick as his temper began to flare. "After everything we've done for you."

"Fuck you, Jerry," Gladys said with a scowl on her face. "You ain't done shit for me."

"You stupid, ugly Bushpig!" Jerry was yelling at her now. He stood in the yard facing her, pointing at her as he spoke. "You try every fucking thing you can to aggravate us. Your attitude sucks and nobody likes that shitty singing you do!"

"Yeah, Jerry, I'm ugly! I look like God! As far as anything you ever did for me, I could put it in my eye."

Suzanne had held back as long as she could. Before she could stop herself, she shouted, "You fucking waste of space.

You piece of shit!" She was shaking, she was so angry. She was defensive, she knew, because Jerry was raising his voice, which was something she'd rarely seen. She wanted to go over and smack Gladys' face. "All you do is sit over there on your fat ass and give us grief." Suzanne thought of her mother, and was glad she wasn't here to see this. She knew that Ruth would've never put up with someone treating Suzanne this way.

"Both of y'all is going to hell. You're going to spontaneously combust! The Lord knows what you're doing to me, and both of y'all is going to hell!" Gladys screamed. Her voice was scratchy and strained. "You're going to learn that you don't tell me what to do. I got more power in my little finger than both of y'all got in your whole body!" Her voice was grating. Suzanne wanted to physically make Gladys shut her mouth, anything to make that voice be silent. Suzanne was disturbed by her own terrible thoughts.

"Fuck you, you stupid fat pig!" Jerry hollered and stomped back into the house and slammed the door. Suzanne paused and went into the house after him, closing the door behind her. "I swear, she's going to make me hurt her," Jerry said. He was breathing hard and his eyes were fierce with anger.

Suzanne looked at him trying to figure out what he would do next. She wasn't sure what she was prepared to do if this situation didn't settle down quickly.

"Listen, Jerry, let's just try to calm down, okay? Maybe they'll put her back in the nuthouse or something," Suzanne said as she patted him on the back.

Jerry looked defeated as he leaned against the doorway. Butterbean was trying to get Jerry's attention by standing on her hind legs and steadying herself against his knee. He bent down to pet her.

Suzanne looked out again, and Gladys was rocking back and forth in the chair on her porch. She looked like she was satisfied with her little outburst and the effect she had on other people. The smug look on her face was too much for Suzanne to look at. She turned her attention back toward Jerry. "Let's get back to work. She's having too much fun aggravating us."

Gladys' singing and preaching went on all day. Between the verses of her songs, she hollered, "Jerry and Suzanne, you ain't going to run me off. I ain't going nowhere!" and "I hate you people! The Lord's going to get you! I'm going to see to it."

"I'll bet the neighbors are just loving this," Suzanne said as she looked out the window.

"Well, they know what we're dealing with here. She'll shut up, eventually."

Suzanne hated what this was doing to them. They had always been a friendly, outgoing couple, and now this situation had turned them into short-tempered, cynical people who couldn't figure out how to react anymore toward their neighbor, or how to function in such a chaotic environment.

A few days later, Suzanne stopped to get the mail as she took Butterbean for her walk. In the mailbox was an envelope with child-like, handwriting. It said <u>To: Jerry</u> on the front. There was no return address on it, but Suzanne had a feeling she knew who had sent it before she even opened the envelope.

Suzanne calmly went into the house without paying special attention to the letter. She knew she was being watched, as usual, from next door. Once inside, she put her purse and keys on the table so she could open it.

The letter said:

Dear Jerry:

You have tried to hurt me, but you are not going to get away with it. Suzanne, you think you are smarter than me, but I know I am smarter than you. The Lord is going to get you for what you have done to me. Jerry, you just want to have sex with me but I won't let you rape me. I think you are trying to kill me. Jerry, the Lord keeps me in the palm of his hand. My husband thought he could kill me, too, but he's the one who ended up dying. You are going to pay for how you have treated me. – Gladys

Suzanne read the letter a couple of times, then put it down, trying to tell herself that it was just crazy talk from a mentally ill woman. She couldn't keep from thinking about it, though. She wanted Jerry to read it so she could get his reaction.

When Jerry got home, she showed the letter to him. As he sat reading it, he looked concerned, but smiled a couple of times. "She's an idiot. Didn't that doctor give you a number to call if Gladys threatened herself or anybody else? Well, I consider this a threat," Jerry said as he reread the letter. "It says 'you are going to pay for how you have treated me'. What's that supposed to mean?"

"Yes, I still have that phone number somewhere." Suzanne went to the desk and retrieved the number from the top drawer. She dialed the number and waited for an answer.

A man answered, "Mental Health Crisis Unit. Can I help you?"

Suzanne explained who she was and what was going on. She stated the purpose of her call to the man and told him that they felt threatened. She asked him if he wanted her to read the letter to him.

"Ma'am, do you know if she has any weapons or has she come onto your property threatening to harm you in any way?" the man asked, ignoring Suzanne's question.

"Well, not yet, but I consider what she said in this letter as a threat. Gladys scares us and we wanted to alert someone that she may be planning to do something violent. She may be capable of doing some very bad things," Suzanne explained.

She could tell her words were having no impact on the man to whom she was talking.

The man sighed and said, "I'm sorry, Ma'am, but unless she's threatening you with bodily harm or wielding a weapon, we cannot respond. I don't know who gave you this number, but it's supposed to be used by family members. I wish there was something we could do to help you, but our hands are tied." His expressionless voice sounded bored as he spoke.

"Of course they are," Suzanne said wearily. "Okay, well, it was worth a shot. Thanks anyway." She hung up the phone and decided to call the police.

The officer who answered the phone transferred Suzanne to a detective that listened to the contents of the letter as Suzanne read it to him.

"Well, she definitely sounds like a nut. But, really, we can't do anything about it unless she tries something. I'm sorry, ma'am. It's a real shame what you're going through there. Listen, if anything, I mean anything happens that can be considered physically threatening, you call us and we'll get out there right away, okay?"

"You don't think this letter sounds like a threat?" Suzanne asked the officer in a desperate tone of voice.

"It sounds like an angry letter from an angry neighbor who happens to be off her rocker. That's about all I can get from it."

Suzanne finished her conversation with the detective with an obligatory thank you. "Jerry, it's the lambs against the wolves, and the wolves are winning."

That night, as Suzanne lay awake trying to make sense of everything that was going on, she heard the slamming of a car door outside the window. She rolled over to look at the time on the clock next to her bed. It said twelve-thirty. For curiosity's sake, she decided to look out the window. There was a hearse that had pulled up to Gladys' house next door. Suzanne squinted as she watched with interest. She wasn't sure if she was completely awake as she watched the driver of the hearse walk up and knock on Gladys' door. Gladys emerged from her house, dressed in her usual several layers of clothing. She had what looked like a man's derby-type hat perched on her head. She walked in a regal manner as the driver escorted her down the sidewalk and into the back of the hearse.

"Alrighty . . ." Suzanne sighed to herself as she lay back down on her bed. She tried to imagine what that was all about, but decided it really didn't matter.

As Suzanne took the dog for a walk the next morning, she ran into her neighbor Chris. After some initial chit chat, Suzanne asked, "Okay, now I just have to ask this. And really, I know it's none of my business, but with all the weird crap going on around here, do you have any idea why a hearse came to pick Gladys up last night?"

Chris laughed and said, "They probably took her to the grocery store. She told me one time that she used to go to church with the funeral director, and they have an arrangement that whenever possible, someone from the funeral home would come get Gladys and take her to the store. She does it at night because she thinks the sun will kill her. You know she's paranoid about the sun, right?"

"Oh, yes, I did know that." Susanne smiled. She thought about how nice it was for the funeral director to allow Gladys to use the hearse for personal errands because she had no other way to get anywhere except by walking. She felt sad that the situation had deteriorated so much that she could no longer help Gladys. Aside from the annoyance, Suzanne had always felt good about helping Gladys. She knew that was a thing of the past, though, and she shrugged off her guilt as she parted ways with her neighbor and proceeded with her walk.

Chapter 16

Jerry began the arduous task of stripping the paint off of the trim throughout the house. He discovered that someone, at some point, had painted a coat of oil-based paint over latex paint, which peeled off in huge strips from the trim. He decided that the only remedy for this problem was to strip and repaint all of the trim with oil paint. It was a huge undertaking since the whole house had the over-sized trim around every window, door, and at the base of every wall.

Suzanne also helped with this project after work and any other time she possibly could. Room by room they went, first peeling as much paint as they could from the trim then using a hand sander to remove the stubborn patches. Jerry then caulked, primed, and repainted each piece of trim in every room.

As the trim was finished in each room, the walls were repaired and painted. The back bedroom was in the worst condition because lifting the house to make it level affected the back part of the house the most. The cracks around the doorway and window were too wide to repair and Jerry didn't want to replace the drywall, so he patched them with drywall mud then hung paneling in the room which was painted to match the rest of the walls in the house.

One evening, as Jerry was prepping a room to be painted, he looked out the window and noticed that there were several cars parked outside Gladys' house. It was unusual to see that much activity next door. He mentioned it to Suzanne at dinner later that night.

"Actually, I've seen more traffic next door, too. Mostly it's in the evening or at night. What caught my attention is that it sort of started out of the blue."

Sitting in her darkened living room that night, Suzanne began to seriously watch what was going on next door. She felt like the nosey neighbor from hell, but this was more than just watching the comings and goings of a few teenagers. There was just something not right about things next door. Suzanne watched as car after car pulled up next door. These were nice vehicles including a Mercedes, a Lexus, and a Cadillac. What in the world would they want over there, Suzanne wondered.

The strange part was that the people dropping by the house next door usually only stayed a few minutes and left. Some of them never even got out of their cars. Frank walked down his front steps to the sidewalk to talk to them. Sometimes, cars with several people inside pulled up, but only one or two went up to the house. The rest stayed in the car listening to music so loud it made the windows buzz with the thumping of the bass.

Frank also began having people come over to his house all hours of the day and night to visit. They mostly hung out in the front room of the house and on the porch. Frank was a sullen young man, and didn't seem to have many friends before this sudden surge of popularity. It didn't make sense to Suzanne.

There was marijuana smoking and beer drinking on the front porch by groups of young people who weren't even attempting to hide their actions. The fact that most of these people looked underage was concerning to Suzanne. "We ought to call the police and tell them that Gladys is giving alcohol to minors," she told Jerry. "The fact that they're over there smoking pot is worse."

"Well, we can't sit up all night and watch these hoodlums party next door. You know that both of us drank beer and smoked pot when we were younger. That's not really the issue. I just don't trust them; that's the part that bugs me. Come on, let's get some sleep and let them get in trouble all on their own." Suzanne felt a little prudish for thinking about calling the police just because they were drinking and smoking grass next door. Maybe Jerry was right, but if things got out of hand, she was determined to report anything and everything that went on next door. She decided to go to bed and think about it in the morning.

Butterbean barked and woke Suzanne from a deep sleep. The dog was growling at a noise coming from outside. Suzanne looked at the clock. It was nearly one o'clock in the morning. She made her way to the window and pulled the blinds apart just enough to look out. There were about five people standing on the porch next door passing a joint around. It was pretty easy to see what was going on because of the lights from inside Gladys' house that were shining through the window and onto her front porch. Suzanne yawned as she watched what was going on.

The people standing around the yard and on the porch next door weren't being rowdy, but they weren't trying to be quiet as they talked either. Suzanne saw one of the guys look around and then walk into her yard. Her heart was beating fast as she moved where she could see out of the front window. There were no lights on in her house, so she was hoping the guy couldn't see her watching him. She was afraid he would come to her front door. Butterbean was growling and Suzanne shushed the dog by tapping it on the nose.

Suzanne watched as the guy walked to a tree in her front yard. He was obviously drunk as he fumbled with the button and zipper on his pants.

Jerry walked up behind Suzanne and saw what she was looking at outside the window. "He's drunk and looking for a place to piss." He pushed Suzanne aside and opened the door.

He walked out onto the porch, which startled the guy about to urinate on their front lawn. Jerry didn't say anything; he just stood there staring at the young man. He hurriedly buttoned his pants and was trying to zip them up as he walked back to the party next door. He kept looking over his shoulder to make sure Jerry wasn't coming off the porch after him.

"Fuckers," Jerry said as he came back in and closed the door. "No respect." He shook his head in disgust. "You know, I don't give a shit what they do over there, except when it wakes me up and I have to work the next day. And here we have another interrupted night of sleep." He made his way through the dark back to his bed. Suzanne heard him tossing and turning, trying to get comfortable. She knew his mind was working overtime and that he couldn't sleep for thinking about what to do.

Suzanne sat on the couch and decided she needed to say a prayer. She asked the Lord to watch over them and to help them be strong until all of this was over. She was so sleepy that she almost fell asleep as she prayed. A sense of tranquility came over her as she lay down on the couch and slept there the rest of the night.

Suzanne saw one of the neighbors while walking Butterbean the next afternoon. "Kathy, something is going on next door. There's an awful lot of partying and visitors at Gladys' house. It goes on pretty much every night. We're losing sleep over this. What do you think it is?"

Kathy, who lived one street over, answered, "If I were you, I'd be real concerned about what's happening next door." The look on her face was serious.

"Why? Do you know what's going on over there?"

"Drugs," the neighbor said matter of factly. "They're selling drugs over there. Everybody knows it but you, I guess."

It finally made sense. The traffic, the well-to-do kids in fancy cars, all hours of the night. "I knew they were smoking pot over there, but I didn't know they were selling it!" Suzanne said.

"It's more than just a little weed they're selling over there," Kathy said in a cautionary tone. She was talking softly, afraid for anyone to hear what she was saying. "There's some bad shit going on over there. It's dangerous to live next to a place like that. You never know when somebody's going to get shot or something. Y'all probably need to call the police. I would if I were you," advised Kathy.

"I see the neighborhood watch is going strong!" a voice yelled loudly from across the street. Suzanne and Kathy turned to see Frank standing on the corner watching them as they talked. He was out of breath and looked agitated although he was smiling. He was leaning over with his hands on his knees as if to steady himself while he got his breath.

Suzanne and Kathy looked at each other, but didn't say anything. Kathy looked worried.

Frank then started laughing hysterically and pointing at them. Then he ran back down the road toward his house, jumping occasionally to hit at low branches on trees lining the sidewalk.

"Okay. Now that was bizarre," Kathy said with a surprised look. "What a weirdo. You guys better call the cops as soon as you can. That boy's got problems. He's probably high on something right now."

"High and crazy. What a combination," Suzanne answered.

Suzanne called the police department the next day to report what was going on next door. She recognized the name of the officer who answered the phone. He had attended one of the neighborhood meetings.

"Well, I guess the best thing for you to do is to get license plate numbers from some of the cars that are driving around over there," the officer advised Suzanne.

"How am I going to do that? I'm afraid of getting caught."

"Oh, I understand that. You'll have to be really careful, but you can do it. I just need a dozen or so. That way I can look them up and see if they belong to anybody who's already in trouble for buying drugs, or selling them for that matter."

"Why can't someone from your department do that? Why should I be the one risking my safety to get this information?"

"To be honest with you, we just don't have enough officers to do that kind of work. We're understaffed right now. That's why we have to have the public's assistance with things like this. And, no, I'm not asking you to risk your life to get this information. The last thing I want is for you to get hurt over this. If you could casually obtain those numbers without being noticed, that would be the best way."

"I guess I could do that. Some of our neighbors know about this, and they've known about it for a while now, but they're not willing to take any action. It's hard to understand why decent people put up with this."

"Fear of retaliation is the main reason. But like I said, just don't get caught checking people out. Be discreet. And if you get in over your head, call the police. Just don't do anything too risky, okay?"

Suzanne began watching for cars to pull up in front of the house next door. She decided she'd take the dog for walks past Gladys' house so she could observe vehicles for descriptions and get license plate numbers. She resented the fact that she had to do the police's work for them, but she was willing to do what it took, within reason, to help make this problem go away.

As she passed each car she made a mental note of the type of car and memorized the license plate number. She repeated the information over and over in her mind until she got back into her house where she immediately wrote it down. She was nervous and worried that someone would notice her looking at their car.

After getting the information on several vehicles over the span of a couple of weeks, she called the police officer back to relay it to him. When Suzanne reminded him of who she was and what she was calling about, he did not remember talking to her in the first place. "Remember, you told me to get this information and call you back with it so you could run a trace on the vehicles?" Suzanne asked.

"Ma'am, I appreciate you getting this information for us, and I'll look into it, but it could be a long time, if ever, before we're able to do anything about it," the officer explained.

Suzanne couldn't believe what she was hearing. "You mean I risked my safety getting those license plate numbers and you're too busy to even look them up? Why didn't you tell me that all of this was for nothing?" Suzanne said. She wanted to cuss the policeman out, but decided that wasn't a smart thing to do.

"We just don't have the personnel to investigate every call that comes through here," the officer told her. "I'm sorry, but that's just the way it is. I'll do my best to look into it for you." He sounded preoccupied and rushed.

It sure doesn't pay to try to change things around here, Suzanne said to herself. Her discouragement seemed overwhelming. What would have to happen before something could be done? Weren't the police there to protect and serve? In real life, Suzanne had learned, it doesn't always work that way. She considered the fact that the police department was understaffed, but citizens weren't allowed to take the law into their own hands. I hope this doesn't come down to self-defense, Suzanne said to herself as she dejectedly tore up the piece of paper with the license plate numbers on it.

Jerry and Suzanne were about halfway through the house remodeling at this point, and they already knew that as long as these people lived next to them, there would never be a happy day in that house. In the beginning, even small projects that were finished seemed like a reason to celebrate. Now, it was just a matter of getting one more thing done. The joy just wasn't there anymore.

About a month later, at one o'clock in the morning, Suzanne and Jerry were awakened to the sound of a slamming door. Suzanne put on her glasses and scrambled to the window, peering through the blinds to see what was going on. Her heart was pounding with anxiety. She saw Frank following two other young teenage-looking guys out of the house down the front walkway to an old beat-up car parked on the street. One of the young men was carrying what looked like a suitcase. He carried it by the handle in front of him, and it appeared to be heavy as he was putting effort into carrying it. The young man behind him was looking around as if to see if anyone was watching them.

"What do you think that is?" Suzanne whispered to Jerry. He had gotten up and took a turn looking out the window.

"I don't know. Maybe it's a big dope deal, big enough to fill a suitcase," Jerry whispered back. He rubbed his stubbly chin and yawned. "Whatever it is, I don't care. Let's get some sleep, okay?"

Suzanne tried to go back to sleep, but her mind was working overtime. She imagined several scenarios of what she witnessed. She envisioned a drive-by shooting and people scattering from the house next door. Surely gunshots would inadvertently hit her house. She imagined seeing the police pull up and arrest Gladys and her son. What if they were found dead over there? She finally fell asleep and dreamed of tornadoes ripping the whole neighborhood apart.

After the incident of the guys taking out the suitcase in the middle of the night, Suzanne and Jerry noticed that the traffic next door stopped. Only one teenage boy was hanging around the house. He and Frank slouched in the two chairs on the front porch next door and stared them down as they came and went. It was uncomfortable and increasingly hard to overlook as they walked past the guys and ignored the menacing stares from them.

Dread filled Suzanne's chest as she came home from work every day. She knew she'd have to walk up the sidewalk to her house past the two young men or Gladys glaring at her. They seemed intent on intimidating her. Occasionally, Suzanne heard Gladys saying things as she walked by, "You're going to leave this neighborhood. I'm going to see to it that you get what you got coming to you."

Suzanne didn't respond or show emotion of any kind. Some days this was hard for her because her feelings were so close to the surface. She wanted to tell Gladys to go fuck herself.

On many nights, the police were parked next door for some type of domestic problem. Suzanne wasn't even surprised anymore when she saw blue lights flashing outside her bedroom window. There were alternating sounds of fighting next door – screaming, crying, cussing, and occasionally crashing noises that sounded like things being thrown in the house.

There were episodes of Gladys throwing Frank out and telling him to never come back, screaming at him as he walked down the road away from the house. This happened at least twice, but he came back both times.

The second time Frank moved back in the house after being told to leave, it was noticeable that his personality was changing. When Jerry and Suzanne first moved into their house, Frank sometimes tried to mediate between his mother and other people when she went into her tirades. But now, it seemed like he was losing touch with reality, too. He couldn't keep a job, he was talking to himself, and he had no friends, except for the teenage boy who stayed at his house from time to time. He was becoming a strange and scary individual.

Suzanne wondered if Frank was on drugs, but he didn't act stoned and he didn't come down. His personality seemed to change before their eyes.

One night at around ten-thirty, Jerry and Suzanne were trying to sleep when they heard loud rap music coming from next door. Of course, they knew who it was. Jerry looked out the blinds to see Frank and the teenager sitting on the porch smoking. The radio was loud and they were just sitting there, not talking or even looking at each other. The music on the radio was distorted with the loud volume.

"I hope they shut that crap off soon. I seriously need to get some sleep," Jerry said as he rolled over and put a pillow over his ears. "I'll give them a few more minutes."

After thirty minutes, Jerry sat up in the bed and said, "Go ahead and call the police."

"Are you sure?" Suzanne asked as she reached for the phone. "I don't want to get a bunch of stuff stirred up. You know they're just doing it to aggravate us. Maybe we should just let it be."

"We have to work tomorrow. They don't. Call the police, please, Suzanne."

Suzanne felt the now familiar pang of fear in her chest as she dialed the number for the police. She knew the number by heart.

When the police car pulled up, the blue lights were flashing. Jerry said, "They're here."

"Should we go out there and talk to them?" Suzanne asked.

"No, let's just wait and see what happens. Let's keep the lights off and stay quiet," Jerry answered in a hushed voice.

"Right. I'm sure they'll never know it was us who called the police," Suzanne whispered and rolled her eyes. "By the way, why are we whispering?"

Butterbean had gotten out of her bed and began growling at the noises. Suzanne knelt down and shushed the little dog before she managed to let out a bark. "Hush now. Go to sleep, baby girl." Suzanne felt sorry for her dog as she led her to her bed. "You go to sleep. Go on, lay down." It seemed that even poor Butterbean was being affected by all of the stress.

Jerry stood at the window facing Gladys' house and watched the policeman as he walked up to the boys on the front porch next door. The officer had a conversation with them, the music was turned down, and the officer left.

Jerry and Suzanne waited and listened. There was no more noise from next door. They climbed back into bed hoping that their drama for the evening was over.

A few minutes later the music was turned back up, as loud as before. Jerry said to Suzanne, "Call the police." He went ahead and got dressed. It was dark in the house. They still hadn't turned on any lights.

"Where are the police?" Jerry was walking nervously back and forth through the house. He knew the guys next door were trying to intimidate him. He wanted to go over there and confront them, but he knew he'd get in trouble if he did, and he wasn't willing to go to jail over some dumb-ass kids next door. "If the police don't get here soon, I'm going to go over there myself."

The police finally arrived. This time it was two police cars. In all, there were three officers who arrived on the scene. The boys turned the music down before the officers got to their porch. "I thought I told you to keep the noise down out here," the officer said in a frustrated tone of voice. He was obviously annoyed that he had to come back out for another disturbance.

Frank was explaining something to the officer that Jerry couldn't hear. The officer said, "I don't care. If I have to come back out here one more time tonight, I'll have to arrest you. If you get smart with me, I'll arrest you now." The officer stood there for a minute to make sure what he said sunk in with the young men. The boys didn't say anything further. The officer then walked toward his cruiser to leave, glancing back at Jerry and Suzanne's house.

Once the police left, Frank's friend left. Frank began pacing across the porch slinging his hands in an agitated way. Gladys had come out on the porch with her cigarettes and said, "Didn't I tell you? I told you about them people." She sat on her green chaise lounge chair and smoked a cigarette, watching her son stomp back and forth across the porch.

"I wish I could kill that mother-fucker!" Frank said with bitterness in his voice. "I wish he'd come out here right now and I would fucking shoot his ass." He was still pacing the small porch like an animal in a cage that was too small. Suzanne could see his face in the glow of the porch light. His expression was more distressed than she'd ever seen it. He looked demented, not focusing on anything in particular.

Frank's temper tantrum continued. "Get the tape recorder and tape this!" Suzanne said to Jerry. Jerry went upstairs to get the tape recorder and came back down to tape what was going on next door. "Should we call the police again?" Suzanne asked.

"I don't know. No, let's don't make this any worse than it already is," Jerry answered quietly. Butterbean growled. She had gotten out of her bed and stood by the door looking out the window. "Shhh. That's a good girl," Jerry whispered as he tried to calm the dog by petting her head.

Jerry slowly opened the door to put the recorder on the porch. "Keep Butterbean quiet. She can't be barking right now. And close the door right after me, but don't close it all the way." He put his finger to his lips and crawled out the door on his hands and knees. The bamboo curtain that they'd placed on the side of their porch hid him as he quietly placed the recorder within recording distance of the noise next door. He then backed up, still in a crawling position on the porch. Suzanne opened the door quietly to let him in.

"If that bitch says anything else to me, I'm going to say, shut up, Bitch! I'll smack that bitch's face." Frank is acting as crazy as his mother, Suzanne thought.

He pulled off his shirt and said, "What's next? Are they going to tell me I can't walk around without my shirt? Fuck that. I wish he'd come out here right now. I would fuck him up. I wish I had a baseball bat, I would crack his head open and his brains would be laying on the fucking ground!" Suddenly, Frank jumped off the side of his porch and walked down the street and out of sight.

"Should we stay up and watch him?" Suzanne asked. She was worried that he'd try to do something to them. She looked at the clock. It was almost midnight.

"No, he won't do anything. He's probably doped up on something, and he just needs to walk it off," Jerry said. He had pulled his shoes off and sat on the side of the bed. "I'll go out there and get the recorder tomorrow morning. It'll shut itself off when it runs out of tape. Let's just try to get some sleep."

Suzanne was exhausted, but couldn't sleep. Insomnia was having an effect on her, and she felt like she hadn't had a restful night of sleep in weeks. She stared into the darkness, thinking about why God had allowed her to get into such a bad situation. Too much work, no money, and no peace of mind. She turned over on her side and sobbed. If her mother hadn't died, would she have stopped Suzanne from making this huge mistake? She tried to picture her mother's face as she lay in the dark room filled with despair. Butterbean whimpered from her bed in the corner of the room. "Go to sleep Butterbean. Everything's okay."

The next few weeks seemed to go by in a blur. Suzanne tried not to let her depression and lack of sleep affect her at work. Her job was the only place she could go for any level of normalcy, and she couldn't afford to lose it. Suzanne had a calendar on her desk. She crossed each day off in red ink.

Each day she was closer to getting out of the miserable situation she'd gotten herself into.

Suzanne decided that she needed counseling to get through this period in her life. When she got to the counselor's office, she waited anxiously in the lobby for her turn. She felt physically sick as she looked at a magazine on the table.

The counselor came to the waiting room and had Suzanne follow her to her office. It was a dimly-lit room with a few table lamps and a narrow window allowing a small amount of sunlight into the room.

Suzanne sat in a comfortable chair across from the counselor, who was a pleasant looking middle-aged woman. The counselor had her hair in a big clip on top of her head that looked neat. Suzanne imagined trying to make the same hairdo work on herself.

"Okay, Miss Suzanne, what's going on with you?" the counselor asked as she opened Suzanne's file.

Suzanne hesitated for a moment, trying to figure out where to begin. She opened her mouth to speak and burst out crying. It surprised both the counselor and Suzanne.

"There are some tissues on the table beside you," offered the counselor. She scooted forward in her seat and looked concerned. "Take your time."

Suzanne composed herself finally and took a deep breath. "I'm just really stressed out right now," Suzanne started. She couldn't look up at the counselor for fear she'd start crying again. She looked down at her used Kleenex. "I live in squalor; my husband and I are trying to finish an old house that we bought to fix up. It's so much hard work. I'm so tired!" Suzanne began crying again. "Wait, I promise I can get through this," Suzanne said as she wiped her eyes and started talking again.

The counselor patiently waited. She had a look of sympathy on her face and listened intently.

"There's this big fat lady who lives next door and I know she's got mental problems, but she's making our lives a living hell. Her son threatens us all the time. We're broke, and my husband is so busy working on this stupid house that he can't break away to get out and get a job that pays money."

"A big fat lady next door who bothers you all the time?" The counselor couldn't hold back a smile. "Go ahead, I'm listening. Your choice of words is rather amusing."

Suzanne wasn't sure if the counselor was making fun of her or not, but she continued. "My husband and I aren't getting along most of the time, and this whole thing is not fair to either of us. Neither of us can walk away. We're both in this mess till the house is finished."

The counselor was writing notes. Suzanne paused, and then resumed talking when the counselor looked up at her. "I can't sleep at night and it seems like I'm in a deep hole I just can't get out of. Oh, and my mama just died a few months ago." Suzanne sighed and sat back in her chair. She felt relieved after getting these words out of her mouth. She would've felt even better if she had some water.

"Wow, you <u>are</u> carrying around a lot of grief," the counselor said as she laid down her pen on the desk. "First of all, you haven't given yourself time to grieve for the loss of your mother. You've jumped headlong into this overwhelming project that you cannot monetarily or physically manage. And now you're really suffering from it. Do you have family and friends you can talk to?" she asked.

"Yes, I have family, but not much. My father is so sad about losing my mother that he's worthless to talk to. My sister works all the time. They live a good ways from me, too. I don't think that's the way for me to turn as far as talking to someone. I do have some good friends at work who are supportive. But listening is all they can do. They can't really help me otherwise. Jerry's family is a huge help. We would have folded a long time ago without their assistance."

"Well, Suzanne, you have several issues that need to be dealt with. There's no way we can address them all today. Let's set up a schedule of appointments for you to come back and talk to me. How does once a week sound?"

"That sounds good, but I can't get away from all the crap I have to do long enough to come see you every week," Suzanne said with tears in her eyes.

"If you don't start addressing these situations, you're going to be sick. You already can't sleep. Make it a priority, okay?" the counselor said with compassion.

"Okay, I'll consider that." Suzanne picked up her purse. "I'll call and make those appointments. You're right. I'm going to lose it if I don't get some help with all of this stuff that's going on in my head."

As Suzanne left her appointment, she picked up a business card at the front desk. When she got to the parking lot, her truck wouldn't start. "Fucking story of my life," Suzanne said as she sat feeling intensely discouraged. She leaned back in her seat and closed her eyes. After taking a few deep breaths, she decided to go back into the building to call Jerry. She saw a man walking out of the building with a cell phone clipped to his belt.

"Sir? Can I use your phone? I'm stranded here," Suzanne asked. When the gentleman handed over the cell phone, Suzanne called home and Jerry answered. "Believe it or not, this bitch won't start. Please come get me."

The gentleman looked surprised when he heard Suzanne's abrasive language.

Suzanne looked apologetic as she turned away from the man to talk. "Uh, I mean, my truck is stalled out."

"I'll be there in a few minutes," Jerry answered.

Suzanne decided not to go back to the counseling sessions. She didn't really have the time to spare, and she felt like as long as she had Jerry to talk to and her friends at work, she'd be okay. She had to admit, though, she felt a little more optimistic about her situation after getting everything off her chest with the counselor.

Trying to have a better attitude toward a helpless situation wasn't easy. Suzanne kept it in her mind that there is a season for everything and that this terrible time of her life would pass sooner or later. These internal mantras became her lifeline of hope. She could handle anything as long as she kept her faith.

Chapter 17

A few days later, when Suzanne got home from work, there was a police cruiser parked in front of her house. She had to drive around the house to the alley and park in the back yard. What in the world is going on now . . . she said to herself as she got out of her truck.

Jerry was in the house watching out the front window.

"What's up? Why are the police here?" Suzanne asked, peering around him to see what he was looking at outside.

"They're not here on account of us," Jerry answered.

"Why are they parked in front of our house then?"

"They're over there talking to Frank. I don't know what's going on, but I think they're planning to take Gladys away," said Jerry.

Suzanne's felt a rush of excitement. She smiled at Jerry. "Do you really think so? How do you know?"

"I don't know for sure, but the officer is over there talking to Frank and I heard the officer ask him if he was ready for this."

There was another lady on the porch talking to Frank and Suzanne recognized her as Gladys' nurse who frequently came by to check on her.

"That's that nurse we see over there all the time. You're right, they may be getting ready to take her away." Suzanne's eyes were open wide. "I wonder if that phone call I made to her doctor has anything to do with this."

"Let's go sit on the porch and watch, but be quiet," Jerry said. He opened the door as quietly as possible and motioned for Suzanne to follow. Suzanne sat in a chair on the front porch and crossed her legs. She wanted to be comfortable as she watched the situation unfold in front of their house. She realized that this was the first time they were able to enjoy the front porch since they bought the house.

The police officers had gone into Gladys' house and minutes later came out escorting her to the police car that sat in front of Jerry and Suzanne's house. Her hands were in handcuffs behind her back. One officer was leading her by the arm and another officer walked slightly ahead and opened the police car door to put Gladys inside.

Jerry had to fight his urge to sit slack-jawed as he watched. Bushpig was in handcuffs! It was just too much. What a scene.

"I ain't never had handcuffs on me before! Take these things off me!" Gladys insisted, trying to wrench her hands out of the cuffs.

"Just calm down and get in the car, ma'am," the officer said flatly.

"I've got to get my pillow. I can't sit on them hot seats, Mister!" Gladys was belligerent as she screamed in the officer's face. He stared back at her with disregard as she spoke. The other officer had already gotten into the passenger seat. He looked on with little concern.

"We'll roll the windows down. Please, just get in," the officer tiredly instructed. He remained courteous as he helped Gladys get into the backseat of the car. The back end of the cruiser noticeably sank with the load of her weight.

Once the car door was closed, Gladys looked up and finally noticed Jerry and Suzanne sitting on their front porch watching her get taken away. Suzanne felt a little smug and even smiled sarcastically at Gladys. She felt like an asshole, but she enjoyed it anyway.

"Do you think they'll keep her forever?" Suzanne asked Jerry as the police car pulled away.

"Maybe. I hope so."

"I'll bet those policemen never had such a stinky prisoner before," Suzanne said. "They probably want to put down all the windows and stick their heads out while they take her to the nut house."

Jerry laughed. They felt a huge sense of relief and celebrated by going out to dinner.

The next day was Saturday, and Suzanne and Jerry were working on some things around the house when they heard a crashing sound next door. Jerry ran to the front room and looked out the blinds in the direction of the noise.

Frank was standing on his front porch looking down at the ground. In the yard, a few feet from the porch, lay the beat-up green chaise lounge that Gladys always sat in, sprawled out on the ground. The cushions were laying about three feet away from the metal frame.

Suzanne looked at Jerry with a smile and said, "Maybe that means she's really not coming back!"

"That's what it looks like," Jerry said. He was smiling, too.

Jerry and Suzanne reveled in the newfound peace with Gladys being gone. They enjoyed themselves doing yard work and sitting on their porch. When Suzanne came home from work, she parked in front of the house and used the front door every day. She felt, for the first time in months, the freedom of coming home without fear of confrontation and intimidation. It was a good feeling.

Frank also kept mostly out of sight for several days. Occasionally, for short periods of time, he sat on the porch in silence staring at the road. He appeared to be unhappy with Gladys gone. It seemed like it took all the energy out of him to be staying alone. It was an eerie peacefulness, but things appeared to be settling down.

One morning, a couple of weeks later, Suzanne was warming up her truck to go to work. As she sat in her truck, she was thinking about the things she had to do at work that day. She casually looked in the rear-view mirror and caught her breath. Was she seeing what she thought she was seeing? There stood Gladys, behind Suzanne's truck, glaring at her through her rearview mirror. "Fuck!" Suzanne said to herself. She watched as Gladys walked slowly back and forth across the street defiantly staring at Suzanne. Gladys had on her nightgown, an oversized man's coat, and fuzzy slippers on her feet.

Suzanne called Jerry from work. "Sasquatch is back. That fucking Bushpig is back!" she said.

"I know. I saw her walking with that pitiful beast she calls a cat this morning," Jerry said with a let down tone to his voice.

"Oh well, I guess it was nice while it lasted," Suzanne sighed. She felt disheartened, but she looked on the bright side. The house was finally in good shape after two years of hard work, and she knew that she wasn't tied to it every minute of the day like she'd been for so long. She and Jerry were not completely finished with it, but the largest projects had been completed. If worse came to worse, she could get out of the house when Gladys began acting up.

Suzanne noticed that whenever she got in her truck to leave, Gladys had begun placing a rickety chair in a position to directly face Suzanne's house. She held a Bible and stared at the house mumbling inaudible words. It looked like she was putting a spell on the house. Nothing surprised Suzanne anymore.

"I noticed that, too," Jerry said when Suzanne mentioned what she'd seen. "Maybe she's putting a curse on us or something. Wait, now I sound like the paranoid one." Jerry laughed.

"Jerry, I know there are no evil spirits in this house, but just for the heck of it, will you do an exorcism on the house with me?" Suzanne asked, her eyebrows raised with anticipation of reproach from Jerry.

"You're kidding, right?"

"Come on, humor me!"

Jerry laughed. "Well, I guess so. Couldn't hurt," he replied with a mocking grin.

"Come on, please take this seriously!" Suzanne said.

They went from room to room, joined hands in each one, and chanted together, "All evil spirits, if there are any evil spirits, are ordered to be gone now." They closed their eyes and concentrated as they chanted.

As they got about halfway through the house, Butterbean came in to check out what was going on. They bent down and held Butterbean's paws as if she was part of the exorcism. Butterbean resisted and chewed at their hands as they held her paws.

Jerry opened one eye to see Suzanne dutifully concentrating on the exorcism. He felt silly, but if it made Suzanne feel better, he was willing to do it. Maybe they'd get a good laugh out of it later. It was a half-hearted effort, but with all the bad luck they'd been having with this house, it seemed a harmless precaution.

When they were finished, Suzanne declared, "Well, that ought to do it!"

"Yeah, that ought to fix everything," Jerry sarcastically answered with a smile as he sat down to pull his shoes off. "I'm so tired. I've got to get some sleep." They finished getting ready for bed and turned out the lights.

Smack! Smack! Jerry woke up and looked at the clock. It was close to midnight. He sat up in bed. Suzanne was already sitting up looking for her glasses. He jumped out of bed and went to the window. Looking next door at Gladys' house, Jerry stood with his mouth wide open.

"What's that noise?" Suzanne asked as she walked to look out the window.

There was Gladys, beating a piece of meat with a tenderizer mallet. It looked like she was going to beat it into oblivion. She turned it over and beat the other side. She had put the meat on a cutting board and was trying to steady it on a chair with one hand, while she whacked it with her other hand. Every time the mallet connected with the meat, a sickening thud echoed. It sounded like it was in the same room with them.

"Goddamn it. A person can't get any sleep around here," Jerry said. "Does she have to do that shit on the front porch?" He started to put his clothes on to go outside to say something, and then everything was quiet again.

Jerry listened and waited. The screen door slammed shut next door. He looked at Suzanne and laughed. "Only Gladys would be out on her front porch beating a piece of meat in the middle of the night!" Suzanne was doubled over laughing. She could barely catch her breath. "Did you see her hair?" Jerry said between bouts of laughter. "She looks like the fucking devil. I guess the exorcism didn't work after all."

"We have got to get the upstairs finished so we don't have to sleep down here next to her front porch anymore," Suzanne said as she finally went to sleep.

Jerry decided it was time to work on the porches on the back side of the house. His first mission was to get a covered porch built over the area where the dirt had been hauled out of the basement. It had been covered by the plastic awning structure for months, and occasionally water made its way into the basement. Something permanent had to be built.

Not having any help made the remaining rehab projects extremely difficult for Jerry. Gilbert was now working at a service station, Robbie Perry had started another project, and no one else was around to lend a hand. He set out to do the job alone.

First, he set the support posts in place with concrete and let them set. He then built a frame and situated the flooring joists. Plywood was then laid for the flooring and a wall was built along the side of the porch that faced Gladys' house to block noise.

As Jerry was working in the back of his house, he noticed Gladys walking around to the back of her house, sitting on her concrete back step. She stared at him as he worked. Curiosity must've gotten the better of her, he thought as he kept his attention on the tasks at hand.

After a couple of days, Gladys pulled a chair out onto her back stoop and started singing. Jerry looked at her and laughed to himself. She just wouldn't give up aggravating him. It seemed as though it had become a sport for her at this point. Jerry kept working and ignored Gladys the best he could.

Jerry built a roof onto the back porch and ran electricity to the ceiling for an outdoor light. Next, he installed an extra window that he'd stored in the basement into the wall facing Gladys' house. Since it was a new window, it needed to be glazed, caulked and painted. Jerry walked to the side of the house facing Gladys to work on it, and he noticed that the windows were all up at Gladys' house. She had air conditioning, so it was unusual to see all the windows up on such a hot day. Jerry continued to work on getting the window caulked and painted.

From next door, music began blasting out the windows. Jerry was startled at first and looked back at Gladys' house. He noticed that the speakers were pointed out the windows toward his house. Jerry kept working, not saying a word, although he was tired and hot, and the music was beginning to really irritate him.

Jerry then realized that it was Frank who had set up the speakers when he saw him adjusting one of them toward the window. He was playing the same song over and over on a record player. Out of spite, Jerry danced a little to the music as he worked.

The blaring music became a routine. Every morning the noise began at eight o'clock and wasn't turned down until nine o'clock at night. By the fourth day of incessant noise, including records being played over and over, church organ music with hollering preachers, and rap music, Jerry told Suzanne it was time to call the police about it.

When the police arrived at their house, they were watching for them in their front entry area. The policeman got out of his car and walked up to their house. Jerry opened the door before the officer had a chance to knock.

"Hello, I'm officer Knowles. There was a call of harassment here?" the officer said as he approached Jerry at the front door.

"Yes sir, please come in," Jerry stood to the side so the officer could enter.

"The people next door are playing their music so loud that we're about to go nuts here," Suzanne explained. "They play it all day long. We've just about lost our patience with them."

"Yeah, I can hear it. Actually, I heard it as I pulled up. It's way too loud," said the officer as he walked over to the window facing Gladys' house and looked through the blinds. "Wow, that's not good. I can understand why you need to put a stop to this."

"What do we do?" Suzanne asked. "She hates our guts, so nothing we say is going to help. If we say anything, it'll only make them want to torture us more."

"You can have a citation issued to her for disturbing the peace, but that'll probably make matters worse. I can go talk to them and tell them they're playing their music too loud. I doubt it'll help, but it's a start. It's really up to you as to how you want to handle it," explained the officer.

"Well, let's not do the citation thing yet. If you could go talk to them and let them know they're breaking the law by disturbing the peace that might help. Maybe they'll listen to you," said Suzanne.

"Okay. I'll be right back." The officer opened the door and walked out of the house and down the sidewalk to Gladys' house. He knocked several times before Gladys came to the door. She was squinting from the sunlight and looked like she was surprised to see a policeman standing there.

Jerry and Suzanne couldn't hear the conversation but saw Gladys pointing toward their house and gesturing animatedly as she spoke to the officer. The officer nodded and said something back to her. He then walked down the sidewalk and back up to their house. The music was turned down.

"I told her that she was disturbing the peace and that if she didn't turn the music down that you two could issue a citation to her for the noise, and she'd have to go to court. She said y'all just don't like gospel music and that the neighbors across the street play music and you never complain about them," the officer said as he pulled a business card out of his front pocket. He wrote something on the back of it.

"Oh, she's talking about the people across the street who have a band. They practice one or two nights out of the week. We can't hear it unless we're outside. There's a big difference between that and her unbearable noise."

"I'm sure you're right about that. Anyway, I told her that they need to tone it down over there. If you decide you want to issue a citation to her, call us back and we'll come out and do that. Sorry, folks, I really am. This is a terrible way to have to live. Bad neighbors can sure make you miserable," the officer said as he reached out to give his card to Jerry. "I wrote down my direct number on the back of the card. Call me if you need me, you hear?"

After the policeman left, the music next door was turned up again, even louder than before. "Maybe she'll get tired of hearing it herself. It must be tearing their eardrums up over there," Suzanne said.

After two more days of the intolerable racket, while Suzanne was at work, Jerry called the officer back and asked him to issue a citation to Gladys. He complied with the request and returned to do just that. Gladys was dumbfounded and irate when she was confronted by the policeman. She cussed the officer as he tried to take down her information for the citation. She walked away from him in the middle of the process, slamming the door in his face. The officer talked loudly toward the closed door, "Ma'am, I'd hate to arrest you today, but that's just what I'm going to do if you don't get out here and cooperate with me." He was clearly exasperated with the situation. "And turn that music down now!" he ordered Gladys. She went into the house and turned it down.

Gladys came back out on the porch crying and gave the officer the information he was requesting. When he was finished writing the citation, he gave a copy of it to Gladys, and walked over to Jerry's house and gave him a copy as well. Jerry thanked the officer.

The noise level went down and though things were tense, Gladys didn't turn the music back up. She continued to sit on her porch screaming the gospel from sunup to sundown. There was nothing they could do about the singing, and Gladys knew it.

Jerry continued to work on getting the back porch completed. He had finished building the covered section of the porch, but there was an area that was essentially a mud hole right outside the kitchen door. Jerry started building a deck off the back of the house that would butt up to the covered porch.

He was proud of his progress and how great it looked, adding more character to the house.

As Jerry worked on the new deck, Elaine came over to help Suzanne paint the inside of the covered porch. They chose to paint the porch a complimentary green to match the green siding on the house. It began to take on a finished look that was quite inviting.

Within the first couple of hours of working, they were surprised to see Frank walk into their back yard. He was careful not to come too close to Jerry as he was cutting some decking material on the saw horses. Frank put his hands on his hips and said, "Y'all are too loud over here. I can't think for all the noise you're making!" He pointed at his head when he made the last statement.

"Frank, I'm using screws on the deck so that I don't make a lot of noise. They're just painting; there's no noise to that," Jerry said annoyed. "I think you're looking for things to complain about."

"I heard y'all hammering, and I'm tired of hearing that shit!" Frank said back to Jerry.

Suzanne paused from painting to face Frank. "You need to go back home, now. We have a right to work over here, which is something you ought to try sometime, and we're not bothering you. You better go home," she said looking directly at Frank. "Besides, y'all are the ones making noise all the time, not us."

Frank stood his ground, shaking his head and smiling.

Jerry leaned against the saw horse and pointed his finger. "Frank, you better get out of our yard. You don't belong here and I don't want to have to hurt you." He wiped the sweat from his brow.

"You can't make me leave," Frank said to Jerry. "I ain't going nowhere." He looked indignant as he crossed his arms.

"Oh yeah?" Jerry said as he grabbed a handful of gravel. "Get the fuck out of here, and don't you ever step foot back into my yard again or I'll take this hammer and bust your skull." Jerry's eyes were wide with anger as he picked up the hammer and drew it back behind him.

Frank jumped to avoid getting hit by the gravel and ran back to his house. A few minutes later, he came back with a brick and threw it at Jerry. The brick rolled on the ground and rested several feet from Jerry.

"You better be glad that didn't hit me," Jerry said, but Frank had turned to run away again. "You throw like a girl!" Jerry hollered at Frank as he ran away. Suzanne was shaking inside from the confrontation. She finished the small area she was painting and put the paint brush down.

Elaine, who had witnessed everything, said, "You two need to get out of here. This is dangerous. They're crazy over there."

"Yep, you're right about that," Jerry said as he sat on the edge of the deck and drank some water.

A few minutes later the police arrived. Apparently, Frank had called the police because Jerry had thrown gravel at him. The officers were understanding to Jerry, but told him not to throw anything else at Frank no matter what. "If he comes onto your property and he won't leave, call us and we'll remove him from your property, by force, if we have to."

Jerry agreed that it wasn't the best move he could have made and said he wouldn't do that again. The officers also spoke to Frank telling him not to go into Jerry's back yard again and warned him that he was trespassing.

One of the officers talked to Jerry for awhile after the other two officers left. "You know, it might be a good idea to get a restraining order against him. At the very least, you should make a report about his threats to you. Do you want me to write up a report?"

Jerry thanked the officer and said he'd think about it.

"What do you think about making an official complaint for the record?" Jerry asked Suzanne that afternoon.

"You know what? I'm just tired of fooling around. I think it would be a good idea. But I don't want the police coming over here to do it. Can we go to the police department to talk to them about it? Things are already so tense around here, it seems like meeting somewhere else would be a safer thing to do."

They called the police department, and the detective suggested they meet at a car lot a couple of streets down from their house. The officer stayed in his air-conditioned cruiser taking down their information as they stood in the hot August sun.

"Now, what purpose will this serve?" Suzanne asked the officer when they were finished giving him the information.

"Well, it's like I told your husband, Ma'am, it just goes on file and it shows a history of problems between you and him. We're not going to go arrest him or anything from this, unless you want to have him arrested; however, if you do that, you'll probably make matters worse. To tell you the truth, he'd be out of jail before you'd even be done filling out the paperwork. Then you'd have to take your time to go to court to pursue the matter. It's up to you what you want to do," the officer explained. "I guess you just have to ask yourselves whether or not that would resolve anything."

Jerry and Suzanne looked at each other. "No, we don't want to have him arrested yet. If you could just get this report filed, that would be enough for now," Jerry answered.

They walked back home in the heat, which made them both weary. "Well, at least we're doing something, right?" Suzanne said as they walked toward their house. She was drained and didn't really want to talk about it anymore.

As they passed Gladys and Frank's house they picked up their pace. Gladys was sitting on her porch smoking a cigarette. She glared down at them as they walked by.

"You're going to see. You're going to get what you got coming to you," Gladys said as she held the cigarette up to her mouth. She took a long drag and blew the smoke toward the sky.

"What a hateful old bitch," Suzanne said to Jerry as they entered their house.

Chapter 18

"**L**ook what this is doing to us!" Suzanne cried one night. "We're at each other's throats. Let's just sell this house and get out of this situation while we're still in once piece." Suzanne was talking between heavy sobs. Earlier in the evening they'd gotten in a fight about money. Stress had finally consumed them to the point where they couldn't get along about anything anymore.

Jerry sat silently and thought about what Suzanne said. "Yeah, I guess you're right. I'm not happy either."

"You can keep Butterbean and go to Florida. I know you'd be happier there," Suzanne said softly, almost in a whisper.

Jerry quickly looked at Suzanne as if he were stunned at her response. "You mean, really go our separate ways?" Jerry asked with a tinge of desperation in his voice.

"I think so. We're not getting along. I can't stand it anymore."

Jerry turned to Suzanne and pointed his finger inches from her face. She gasped with surprise. "You ever try to leave me again, and you'll be leaving in a pine box, you hear me?" he hissed at her. He lowered his finger away from her face and looked at her with tears in his eyes.

Suzanne was paralyzed with shock and disbelief. She stared at Jerry not knowing what to expect from him next. Jerry was breathing hard and turned to sit on the side of the bed with his back to her. He began to cry, quietly at first, then with deep sorrow that seemed to completely fill the room. Suzanne was uncomfortable witnessing this pathetic sight, her best friend whose spirit was shattered. She had stopped crying herself, almost feeling numb to her own feelings at this point. All she wanted to do was help Jerry gain control of himself.

Reaching her hand out to touch his back, Suzanne felt him shrug her off. She wanted to comfort him as he began to rock back and forth crying. He was inconsolable and refused to look at her.

"I can't take this anymore. I can't take this anymore. Lord help me!" Jerry sobbed as he placed the palms of his hands on the sides of his head. "My head is killing me," Jerry moaned. "The stress of all this bullshit is killing me."

"Listen, Jerry, I didn't mean it. Come on now, it hurts me to see you this way. Please calm down," Suzanne pleaded. She tried again to reach out to soothe him. She wanted to take back what she said. She went to get a tissue for Jerry. She knelt in front of him; his hands were over his face.

"Jerry, please listen to me. We'll take care of each other and get through this. Please don't cry, this is tearing me apart. Here, take this and wipe your eyes. Please."

Jerry reached out for the tissue and wiped his face. "You don't love me anymore. You probably never did. I know you don't want to be with me."

"Please, let's just don't talk about this anymore tonight. Let me get you something to drink," Suzanne offered as she sat next to Jerry and put her arm around his shoulders. "Okay?"

"Yeah, I could use some water," Jerry said as he laid down on the bed.

"I'll be right back."

When Suzanne got back to the bed with Jerry's water, he was already asleep and snoring. With a sigh of relief, Suzanne lay down on the other side of the bed and tried to rationalize what was going through her mind. Jerry was right. She wasn't in love with him anymore, and hadn't been in years. But she had a strong devotion to him and vowed that night to stick beside him with no more discussion of breaking up for a while.

Jerry and Suzanne made a mutual decision to sell the house as soon as they were finished with it. Regardless of the work involved, they couldn't afford to live there, their marriage had fallen apart, and the neighbors were torturing them. It was a tough decision to make, but the thought of finally being free of this torment actually gave them a goal. Whenever things got too scary, Suzanne would think, as soon as we're finished with this place, we can sell it and leave.

Jerry had conceded, without verbally admitting to an inevitable split with Suzanne, that he was ready for the situation to be over, one way or another. Besides, he owed his parents a fortune since they had financed almost the whole house project from the beginning. The house needed to be sold to pay them back. It was the best, and really, the only solution. He toyed with the idea of getting a loan to pay his parents back so that he could stay in the house he'd worked so hard on, even if it meant staying there alone without Suzanne. After heavy consideration, however, he knew he really couldn't afford everything by himself. And he knew he'd always be miserable there. He began to force himself to think of the positives of getting rid of the house. After a while, he wasn't forcing himself anymore. He realized that he could be happier elsewhere.

Since the downstairs was complete and the front porch had been leveled and shored up, the only part of the house that remained unfinished was the upstairs. Suzanne had received eight thousand dollars from her mother's death. She decided to use the money to finish the upstairs. It was a difficult decision to make, but she saw it as a way to buy her freedom.

Jerry hired some drywall professionals to come and mud and tape the newly-hung drywall. He felt encouraged as things started taking shape. He found himself whistling as he cleaned up the work areas at night, picking up tools and sweeping the floors.

Suzanne stayed up late several nights to finish painting the upstairs trim. She looked around the upstairs, and it was starting to look good. Jerry had torn down the low-hung ceiling and replaced it with drywall that followed the pitch of the roof, making the area look huge. One of the two large rooms in the attic area was made into a large bathroom with a marble double-vanity sink. The other became a spacious bedroom with two pretty windows that drenched the room in sunlight. The back area of the attic that was too short for anyone to stand up in was turned into a long, wide closet.

Once the drywall was completed and painted, new carpet was laid throughout the upstairs. Suzanne called home from work the day the carpet was scheduled to be installed. Jerry answered the phone. "Well? Is the carpet down yet?" Suzanne asked.

"Just about," Jerry answered, sounding excited.

"Well? How does it look?" Suzanne wasn't able to hide her anticipation.

"It looks phenomenal," Jerry answered with a laugh. "They already laid the bedroom carpet. Now they're working on the bathroom area. It's a great color." They had picked out a neutral color with multi-colored flecks of blue and maroon threads throughout. "I can't wait for you to see it."

"I'm going to lie down and roll all over it when I get home, so get ready!" Suzanne said.

"Well, I might have to miss that. I've got to run and bid on a job so we can get more money coming in, so I probably won't be here. But roll on the floor to your little heart's content," Jerry teased.

When Suzanne got home, she ran upstairs to see the nearly-finished rooms. "Oh, my gosh! It's beautiful!" Suzanne exclaimed, even though no one was there to hear her. She sat on the top step of the stairs and looked around her. "This looks so good!" she said with a big smile.

Was this the same uninhabitable area that they practically dismissed when they first saw the house? She wanted to cry with happiness. She sat on the floor and looked around at the progress for a long time, drinking in the smell of the new carpet. She thought about how the bed could finally be moved upstairs and they could have some tranquility at night when they went to sleep. Surely it would be quieter than the downstairs room where they had been sleeping.

Jerry's parents came to visit for several days, and he was excited to show them his progress. He was proud as he led them through the house and pointed out the various projects that had been finished. His parents had always been so supportive, and they seemed impressed with the way the house was shaping up.

True to their nature, they pitched in and helped with some of the tasks that were still unfinished. As Suzanne was working on repainting the front screen door, Jerry and his father were busy re-glazing the outside of the windows. Jerry's mother was working on the plants in the house that had almost died from all the construction dust and neglect. She cleaned each leaf and gave the plants a good misting. Suzanne thought about how sweet it was to have these dear people do what they could to help. It gave her a sense of gratitude that she'd never felt before.

Next door, Gladys had begun singing and preaching earlier that morning. It had started out loud, and as the morning went on it got even louder and more persistent. Jerry and his father could barely hear each other talking. Jerry's father was a minister, and he grimaced as he heard the condemnations coming from next door.

Gladys went inside and got her radio, came back out onto her porch and turned it up as loud as it would go. The music was so raucous it was crackling through the tired speakers. It was gospel church music with an organ background and a screaming singer. Gladys swayed back and forth, slapping her thighs. She had on a big muumuu housedress and knee socks with slippers on her feet.

After about forty-five minutes of the noise, Jerry came down off the ladder and approached Gladys. "Gladys! Hey, Gladys!" Jerry hollered to get her attention. "My mom and dad are here, and we'd really appreciate it if you could turn down your radio."

"You go to hell, Jerry!" she screamed at him. She turned the radio up and continued to rock back and forth in her chair.

"Come on now, please be nice about this."

"Fuck you! You ain't telling me what to do!"

Jerry's anger surged inside him as he looked to see his parents watching the scene with confused expressions. With determined strides, he went into the house to the bookcase where he picked up the aerosol horn he'd gotten to take to basketball games. He turned to go back outside. He was so angry he felt like he could kill somebody. Suzanne tried to stop him as he stormed out the door.

"Jerry, please, don't do this! Don't!" Suzanne was grabbing Jerry's arms. He pulled away from her and kept walking.

Jerry angrily stomped across his yard over to Gladys' house where she was sitting on her porch facing the street. She was still screaming the gospel, her eyes deliberately focusing on anything but Jerry.

Jerry put the air horn about three inches away from her ear and let it rip. The sound was so shrill, it hurt Suzanne's ears, and she was standing several feet away. Jerry pressed the button for several seconds. Gladys ignored Jerry and kept singing. Jerry was cussing her as he squeezed the air horn,

"You sorry, ugly, filthy bitch. You can't stand for anybody to be happy, can you?"

He finally stopped blowing the horn and calmly walked back home. Gladys looked dazed. She had quit singing, although her radio was still blaring. Her body seemed frozen with her hands resting on her thighs.

"Gladys, please let us have some peace and quiet. That's all we want. Can't we stop fighting all the time?" Suzanne felt tears welling up as she tried to reason with the woman. The situation had gotten so out of hand that it seemed that no amount of order could be salvaged.

With an arrogant look of superiority, Gladys turned to glare at Suzanne with unmistakable loathing. Without saying a word, she stood up from her chaise lounge and turned her back to Suzanne. She then pulled up her housecoat to reveal her naked rear-end. After bending over and ceremoniously showing her bottom to Suzanne, she casually straightened up and sauntered back into her house.

Suzanne was shocked, but she decided not to give Gladys the satisfaction of knowing it. Instead, Suzanne looked at the ground for a moment then went back into her house.

I've been mooned by this crazy woman, Suzanne thought. What was the use of trying to make things better?

Suzanne asked Jerry when he came back into the house, "Did you see what she did? She showed her ass to me!"

"And you lived to talk about it?" Jerry said. He looked revolted and amused at the same time. "I'm sorry about being out of control out there. She makes me so mad I just can't stand it. I promise, I won't do that again."

Suzanne studied Jerry's face for a minute before speaking, noting his change in attitude from just moments before. He seemed relieved after confronting Gladys. She took a deep breath and slowly let it out. "I understand, Jerry. It's okay. I'm sorry any of this is happening."

Jerry smiled and winked at her.

As Jerry's parents packed their car to leave the next morning, they lingered for a while to provide a little extra encouragement to Jerry and Suzanne.

"You guys work hard. Get out and have some fun, too, okay? Get away from this house and spend time with friends. Do whatever you need to do to get your mind off this place," Jerry's mother said as she pulled the couple close for a hug.

Jerry's father was walking toward the house to get the last suitcase when he stopped and bent down. He was looking under the back porch. Suzanne watched him, wondering what he was doing.

"What's this?" he said as he reached under the edge of the porch.

Suzanne started walking toward her father-in-law and before she could manage to say anything, he had reached under the porch and was pulling something out from under the steps.

At first, all she could make out was yellowish-orange fur. It took a moment before she realized what it was. "Hey, it's a dead cat!" Jerry's father said, holding it up in the air by its tail.

"Whoa, whoa . . . wait a minute. Put it down. Hurry!" Suzanne was motioning for him to lower the cat.

"Whose cat is it?" he said as he lowered it to the ground.

"Jerry, come here." She waved him over. "It's L'il Tom. It's Gladys' cat!"

"Oh, shit. Dad, we have to get that thing in a trash bag or something."

"What's the big deal?" Jerry's dad was confused as to why there was so much drama.

"Gladys will say that we killed that stupid cat and it won't be pretty, believe me."

"Oh, that's nonsense. You wouldn't kill her cat, for goodness' sake."

"I know that, and you know that. But remember, she's a nutcase."

Jerry came out of the house with a trash bag. "Hurry, stick it in." It almost seemed humorous as he held the bag for his dad to stuff the cat with rigor mortis into it. It was stiff as a board.

A few weeks later, Jerry's sister, Darlene, and brother-in-law, Kevin, came to help with the installation of the upstairs bathroom fixtures. The mood in the house was light as Jerry and Kevin went from project to project. As each thing got done, Suzanne felt as if a weight had been lifted from her shoulders. She had fewer things to worry about and was grateful to Jerry's family for all of their help.

The tour of historic homes was announced at the next neighborhood meeting. It was to be held in October, which was two months away. Jerry looked at Suzanne and they both smiled. They'd almost gotten the house finished to the point of maybe having their home in the tour. If they wanted to be included in it, they would have only two months to finish everything. The thought of having their efforts recognized and appreciated was exciting. The tour could also be the first opportunity for their house to be seen by prospective buyers.

They began in earnest working on the final touches of the house. They finished the upstairs area except for the railing around the stairs opening. They also began putting their belongings away. The entire time they had lived in the house, most of their personal items were still boxed up in the back room. Finally, they could unpack after two years.

Elaine and Paul came to help prepare the house for the historic homes tour. Suzanne felt frenzied because there was so much to do in such a short time, but the help from her family got her through periods of feeling overwhelmed. There was a lot of cleaning and organizing to be done.

Suzanne asked the neighborhood association if it would be okay for her to tell the visitors that the house was for sale. They agreed it was okay as long as there wasn't a "for sale" sign in the front yard. Suzanne decided to design a tasteful flyer to place on the table in the dining room along with the before-and-after pictures on display.

When the day came for the tour, Elaine arrived early at Jerry and Suzanne's house to help them get ready. Right down to the very hour that the tour was to begin, they were taking care of last-minute details and cleaning. Jerry opened the front door for the tour to begin.

The first influx of people came through the door in a large group. They weren't together, but they all arrived at the same time. As they came in the door, Elaine and Suzanne greeted them. "Hello! Welcome! Come on in," Suzanne said as she met everyone entering the house. "This house was built in 1914, and when we bought it, it was almost ready for demolition. Here we are, two years later, finally finished with it!" Suzanne said smiling. People nodded and raised their eyebrows showing their appreciation as Suzanne described some of the work that went into bringing the house back to life.

"These are our before and after pictures on the dining room table." Suzanne motioned as she led the groups through the dining room.

All of the comments were good and the visitors were in awe of the amount of work that had gone into rehabbing the house. There were many compliments on the beautiful floors and the quality of the restoration. People were genuinely pleased with what they saw, and Suzanne felt pride for the results of their hard work. She was so relieved to finally have someone see and appreciate what she and Jerry had done.

After about an hour, the flow of people slowed. Jerry had been showing the back part of the house while Suzanne and Elaine showed the front rooms of the house. During one of the slow periods, Jerry came to the front room where Elaine and Suzanne were standing. This was the first opportunity they had to talk since the tour began. "Well, Jerry, we finally did it," Suzanne said smiling big. With emotion she hadn't felt in a long time, she extended her hand toward him.

"Yes, we did," Jerry said. He reached out and held Suzanne's hand. He had tears in his eyes, but quickly straightened himself up since Elaine was there. He felt an intense sense of accomplishment. This was a special day that was a long time in coming.

Chapter 19

fter the tour was finished at the end of the day, the neighborhood association members got to tour each others' houses. They hadn't been able to do this during the day since they had to stay and greet the people coming in their homes for the tour.

When the group finally got to Jerry and Suzanne's house, they couldn't believe their eyes when they walked in the door. Most of them hadn't seen the inside of the house since it had been purchased, and none had seen it since it had been remodeled.

The main entry room, as was the rest of the house, was freshly painted a creamy vanilla color. All of the extra-wide trim had been stripped and repainted a crisp white. The contrast of the color of the walls and the bright white trim came off looking clean and tasteful. As in all of the downstairs rooms, the newly-laid hardwood floors gleamed. The neighbors couldn't believe this was the same house.

As the group filed into the house, the next room they entered was the dining room with the tiger oak fireplace. Two beautiful mahogany bookcases stood on either side of the floor-to-ceiling window. A new light fixture, resembling an old weathered chandelier, hung in the center of the room. Suzanne had purchased flickering bulbs that looked like candlelight for the fixture. The light danced against the walls and made the room look elegant. Suzanne and Jerry had purchased a large stained-glass window several years before. They had hung it on the wall, which added a touch of antique charm to the room.

The kitchen was the next room to be viewed. The large dimensions of the room captured everyone's attention.   Since the pantry and the old back porch had been incorporated into the kitchen, it was twice the size it used to be. The appliances that Suzanne had scrubbed clean of construction filth now sparkled. Pale green cabinets spanned the length of the long L-shaped counter. Jerry and Suzanne had purchased fancy trim to highlight the cabinets, which made what would've been rather plain looking cabinets look stylish and ornate. New light fixtures shown brightly, making the room feel friendly and warm.

The next area that the group toured was the basement. Some of the neighbors chose not to go down the steep steps to the basement, but most were anxious to see what had been done. As they came down the newly-constructed steps, they were surprised and amazed at what they saw. A concrete floor, all new support posts, a finished laundry area, and eight-foot ceilings completed the picture where only dirt used to be.

"Jerry, how in the world did you do all of this?" asked one of the neighbors.

Jerry explained most of the work that had gone into the rebuilding of the house was the foundation and joist system. This was the heart and soul of the house and the most important part of the entire rehabilitation.   Without the proper construction of this area, the epicenter of the entire project, the rest of the rehab wouldn't have been a success.

After looking at the basement, the group went back to the main floor and on to the next room, which was a bedroom. Everyone worked their way through the doorway to see what had been done to it. Because there had been so much damage to the drywall in this back room when the house was lifted, Jerry had hung wood paneling on the walls, which he finished off beautifully by painting it the same vanilla color that was on the rest of the walls. The simplicity of keeping the same color scheme throughout the bottom floor made the already spacious home seem even bigger.

Suzanne had purchased an old iron bed from a salvage store and a beautiful antique-looking bedspread and curtain to match at a yard sale. Along with the old sewing machine cabinet that Suzanne had inherited from her grandfather, which Suzanne set up as a bedside table, the room was inviting and looked like a page right out of history.

The next room was just another square room that could have been a bedroom, office or flex room. Jerry had added a closet to the room for storage. The only furniture that sat in the room was a rocking chair and a drafting desk. It looked large with the sparse furnishings. Suzanne had placed a big green plant in the room on the desk, along with an antique lamp. The simple room was a hit, as well, with the neighbors.

Next was the bathroom that Suzanne presented with pride. She was especially pleased with the work she'd done on the claw foot tub. The magnolia wallpaper looked bright and was the only wall color variation in the entire downstairs, so it seemed to come alive with vivid shades of green and white. The oversized mirror with beveled edges and gold frame was just the right touch above the fancy, antique-style pedestal sink.

The final room downstairs was the large living room which was beautifully decorated with an oriental rug in the center of the floor. The furniture in the room lent itself well to the overall style of the home. The green and white couch had large comfortable pillows with a floral print. French doors led the group back into the first room they had come to when they entered the house. The comments were all positive and Jerry and Suzanne felt elation at their success.

"Do you guys want to go see the upstairs now?" Jerry asked.

"Lead on, Jerry. Let's see what else you two have done to this place."

"Okay, follow me. Hold on to the rail as you come upstairs. It's a little steep," Jerry said as he led the group up the steps.

The original steps had been covered with new berber carpet as was the entire upstairs. When they got to the second floor, the considerable size of the master suite was revealed. The ceiling that followed the roofline made it appear even more expansive.

Right away, it was noticed that the upstairs area was more contemporary than the traditional looking downstairs of the home. There was a bed with a colorful bedspread and a table on each side of the bed serving as nightstands. An overhead fan was running, giving the room an airy feel. One entire side of the upstairs was closet area. It was spacious and ideal for clothing and storage.

On the other side of the stairway was the master bathroom. It was as big as most people's living rooms. There was a double-vanity marble sink with a wide mirror hanging over it. Suzanne had polished all of the sink hardware and the mirror, making the bathroom look pristine. An extra-large shower, the biggest one that could be brought up the steps during construction, sat in the corner. A commode was tucked away behind the shower area and had a pocket door that provided privacy.

The upstairs was painted all one color just like the downstairs. It made the rooms tie in together well and added a feeling of continuity.

As the neighbors took all of this in, they weren't shy with their praise. Jerry and Suzanne didn't get tired of saying "thank you" all night. They were riding high on the feeling of accomplishment.

After the tour of the remaining homes, there was a potluck dinner for the exhausted homeowners who had presented their homes in the tour. Everyone ate and relaxed as the evening came to a close. It had been a big day, satisfying to everyone involved.

Jerry and Suzanne collapsed into bed that night, each immersed in their memories of the day's events. They both felt good about their success and went to bed with optimistic feelings.

The next morning, Jerry called Suzanne at work to tell her that Gladys' house was being scraped to be repainted. "Are you serious? Who's going to paint it? Is her son out there actually working on that place?"

"It's some kids from a church who do volunteer work, and they're about halfway done scraping it," Jerry answered. "I talked to one of the guys, and he told me that this is part of the missionary work they do to help people in need."

Suzanne was so glad to hear that something was going to finally be done to Gladys' house. It was the biggest eyesore in the neighborhood. At least if it was painted, it wouldn't be so shabby looking.

When Suzanne got home, the kids were still scraping on the house next door, and they were about almost finished. Suzanne walked up to her front door with great satisfaction. She had a good feeling about being able to sell their house.

The next afternoon, Jerry again called Suzanne at work. "You won't believe this." His voice was tight with anger.

"What?" Suzanne asked.

"They're painting the house next door."

"I figured they'd start painting it today . . ."

"Guess what color it is," Jerry interrupted her.

"I'm afraid to ask," Suzanne said. She knew Jerry was about to ruin her day.

"Neon yellow. Suzanne, its fucking neon yellow! And the shutters are black. It looks like a giant bumblebee. It's absolutely the ugliest thing I've ever seen. We'll never sell our house now. Nobody would buy a house next to that."

Suzanne thought he must be exaggerating. Yellow houses seem bright in the beginning, but surely it wasn't as awful as he was describing. Anything was better than the old, peeling paint that had been begging to be scraped off that house.

When Suzanne got home, she couldn't believe her eyes. Gladys' house was the brightest neon yellow she'd ever seen. It practically glowed and pulsed with color. She got out of her truck and stared at it. She was flabbergasted. The neighbor across the street was outside doing yard work. He just looked at Suzanne and shook his head. It really was as bad looking as it could get. The neighbor laughed at Suzanne's reaction.

"Is she fucking retarded or what?" Suzanne said to Jerry when she got into the house. "You're right. We'll never sell this house sitting next to that thing! It's so ugly!" Suzanne slumped in a chair feeling defeated. Butterbean jumped into her lap. "I just don't get it. The harder we work to make our place better, the harder she works to screw it up."

When the church kids came back the next day to finish painting the shutters, Jerry got a young man's attention and asked him, "Why did you guys do this? Why did you paint her house this color?" He tried not to sound annoyed, but knew that he did.

The young man stopped painting so he could look at Jerry as he spoke. "That's what she asked for," he said apologetically. "We hated to paint it this crazy color, especially after working on it as hard as we did, getting it prepped and all. But we gave her some paint samples, and that's the one she picked. Man, I'm really sorry." The young man turned back toward the shutter he'd been painting. Jerry shook his head and walked back home.

"Hey, are you feeling okay?" Suzanne asked Jerry when he got back into the house.

"Yeah, I guess so. I just can't get rid of this headache," Jerry answered.

"It's probably from looking at that neon masterpiece next door," Suzanne said smiling. Jerry didn't acknowledge her statement; he just sat in a kitchen chair massaging his temples.

"It's stress. I'll be fine," Jerry said as he closed his eyes and tried to rest. "If that fat-ass next door sings one more song today, I'm going to go over there and punch her lights out." Jerry kept his eyes closed as he spoke and he was asleep within minutes.

Chapter 20

O ne of the last details Jerry had to finish was painting the side area of the front porch. Jerry and Robbie had rebuilt the porch from the ground up with new supports and flooring. Suzanne had painted most of the materials for porch before they were actually laid into place, but there was one small side area that still needed to be painted. Of course, it was the side facing Gladys' house.

Jerry was on his knees painting the area and was about halfway through when he heard Gladys' screen door open with a moan and slam shut. He never turned around, but he smelled her cigarette smoke and knew that she was standing there watching. He didn't pay her any attention and concentrated on finishing his job.

He heard the screen door slam again and breathed a sigh of relief that Gladys had gone back into her house. A minute later, the door opened again and Gladys had a broom in her hand. Her cottonwood tree had rained a large amount of cottony wisps down onto her porch, which she began sweeping toward Jerry as he painted. He paid no mind to her and kept working. He was determined to get one thing done outside without arguing about it.

When Gladys saw that she was being ignored, she walked down her front steps and began sweeping her yard with her broom. The dirt and cotton were flying everywhere and getting in Jerry's paint and up his nose. He tried to position himself between the debris that was being thrown into the air and the side of the porch he was painting, but it did no good. Gladys started singing loudly as she swung her broom. Pieces of cotton were sticking to the wet paint, and Jerry just couldn't stay quiet about it anymore.

"Gladys, can't you wait a couple hours till this paint dries? Then you can sweep the whole street if you want to," Jerry said in the nicest tone of voice he could muster.

"I'll sweep anytime I want to, Jerry, and you can't tell me what to do," she said in a gruff voice, leaning the broom against her big body. She was waiting for an answer, but she didn't get one. Jerry kept working. She started sweeping again, working her way closer to him.

"I asked you nicely, Gladys, please let me finish this job," Jerry started as he stood up to face her. He had the roller pan full of paint in one hand and a paintbrush in the other.

"Who do you think you are? You can't tell me what to do, Jerry. I've been living in this neighborhood for twenty years, and you've only been here for two years. You ain't telling me what to do." Her voice was raised and she was shaking the broom at Jerry. She looked puffed up with self-righteousness. Her hair was fashioned in what had become a familiar look -- little pony tails all over her head. Jerry wanted to laugh at how ridiculous she looked in her over-sized bedclothes that she was wearing in the middle of the day and her crazy hair style, but he was so mad he said all he could think to say.

"Fuck you!" he said in her face.

"Naw, Jerry, fuck _you_!" she hollered back, her face screwed up with anger. "Go straight to hell! I hate you fucking people!"

"Fuck you," Jerry said in an emotionless, flat tone as he turned back toward the porch to continue his work. He knelt down to finish painting the bottom of the porch area. Gladys kept yelling at him, but no matter what she said, Jerry replied, "Fuck you." He said it about a dozen times using the same monotone voice, showing her no more attention other than to say, "Fuck you." It went on for several minutes before Gladys became frustrated and stomped back into her house. Jerry smiled and started whistling. He didn't let her get to him and he felt really good. He was going to finish the porch that day after all.

Another Saturday came around, and Suzanne was cleaning the house in case any prospective buyers called. She was getting out the vacuum cleaner and saw some movement out the window that caught her eye. She parted the blinds a little more so she could see what was going on.

Outside, Frank was using a five-foot chain to gauge the mid-point between his and Jerry and Suzanne's house. He laid the chain on the ground, straightened it out, and stooped down to see if it was in the middle of the two houses. He then adjusted the chain as he studied it and began digging a trench. Because of the recent rains, it was starting to look like a big, muddy ditch in the front and side yards.

"Jerry!" Suzanne ran to the back of the house where Jerry was working. "You better come see this. The dumb-ass next door is digging up the yard!"

"What?" Jerry said as he ran toward the front of the house. He looked out the blinds and saw Frank digging away. "What a stupid idiot. Call the police. I've worked so hard on that yard, and he's going to make a big mess out of it. It's hard enough to sell this place as it is, thanks to their sorry asses, but if he tears the yard up . . ."

Suzanne called the police and the dispatcher assured her that the police were on their way. "Calm down. We can't do anything till they get here."

Jerry watched out the window. "Where are those police?"

Frank was still lining up the chain and digging.

A few minutes later, Jerry said, "Call the police again. I'm about to go hurt that boy."

Suzanne called the police again, and the dispatcher once more told her that the police were on their way.

A few minutes later, with the anxiety of another confrontation looming, they cautiously walked out onto the front porch. A neighbor was walking down the sidewalk and called Jerry over. Reluctantly, Jerry went to talk to the neighbor. Surprisingly, from what Suzanne could hear, the neighbor was talking about something totally unrelated to what was going on.

Suzanne was relieved to have Jerry occupied for a few minutes, but she was getting anxious for the police to get there. She stood on the porch looking down at Frank digging up the yard. She knew he saw her, but he paid her no attention. Jerry watched the scene as he spoke to the neighbor on the sidewalk.

Finally, Suzanne said, "I didn't know you had a surveyor's license." Frank ignored her. "Do you have a surveyor's license?"

Frank stopped digging for a minute and looked around. "Is somebody talking to me?" he said sarcastically.

"Yes, I'm talking to you and you know it. Why are you messing up the yard like this?" Suzanne asked.

"I'm showing you where the property line is. You don't come over here and I won't go over there," he said, leaning on his shovel looking up at Suzanne.

"You don't have the right to do that and you're making a mess. Besides that, we don't go into your yard," Suzanne answered. "You don't know where the property line is anyway."

Suzanne walked down the front steps of the porch and sat on some rocks that outlined a flower bed in the front yard. She kept talking. "You're not making anything better by digging up the yard."

Frank stopped digging and said to Suzanne, "You are an evil person. When I look at you, I'm looking at the devil." He had a sickening smirk on his face, half-smiling.

Jerry was still watching the interaction out of the corner of his eye. The neighbor he was talking to seemed to have an endless amount of conversation about something. "I'm the devil? ME? Every day when I come home, I have to see either you or your mama staring me down as I walk up the steps to my house. We've had to stand by and watch you sell drugs out of your house. Don't tell me you didn't do that, because I know you did. How dumb do you think we are?" Suzanne felt a sense of relief and power as she spoke. She used as much restraint with her voice as possible, but she felt the need to get it all out. "You've made us miserable ever since we moved here, never a minute's peace. If it's not you causing trouble, it's your mother. And you have the ugliest house in the whole neighborhood!" Suzanne said. It felt good to say what had been on her mind for so long.

"Get out of here and leave me alone," Frank said as he kept digging. He was pushing the shovel into the newly sown grass. Suzanne cringed as she thought about the hours that Jerry had spent working on the yard, sewing grass seed and watering it every night.

"Get out of our yard if you're going to dig," Suzanne said as she crossed her arms.

Frank moved over to his side of the trench he was digging. Finally, the police came driving up the street. Frank threw down the shovel and walked to a neighbor's house halfway down the block. Suzanne watched as he knocked on the neighbor's door. A woman came to the door and a conversation took place. She saw them staring at her as they talked.

Two police cars had arrived on the scene. The officers got out of the car and walked up to Jerry who had finally broken away from talking to the man on the sidewalk.

"What's the problem here?" the officer asked as he looked at the lawn damage.

Suzanne explained what was going on. One officer walked down to the house that Frank had fled to and escorted him back to the area that he'd been digging. He was slouched over as he walked, the officer prodding him along.

Frank tried to explain what he was doing, and the officer listened without interrupting. "Listen, son, don't dig anymore unless you have an official map showing that you're digging on your property. Do you have such a map?"

"No," Frank answered looking defeated.

"Well, then you can't dig anymore. Is that clear?"

Frank turned and walked back to his house without answering. He sat on the porch steps watching the policeman talk to Jerry and Suzanne.

"I know you guys have had a lot of problems with these people. But even before you came to live here, there were a lot of disturbances at their house," the officer explained.

"I think Frank has been in trouble in the past, and he has a bad temper, so we're pretty cautious about him. He knows it, too. The other day he walked past our house pointing and laughing because he knew we were watching him. He gets a kick out of it," Suzanne said.

"It's hard to figure out people like him and his mama. Yes, Frank has been in some trouble," the officer caught himself before revealing any confidential information. He cleared his voice, "Uh, please don't mention that I said that to you," he said in a low tone of voice as if he were telling a secret.

"We're concerned about retaliation from them. I'm afraid they'll burn our house down while we're gone," Jerry said.

"Well, all I can say is call us if it gets scary around here," said the officer as he headed to his car. He pointed to the for sale sign in the yard. "I'm sure you'll sell this house soon and get away from these people." He closed his patrol car door, started his engine and left.

"Now what?" Suzanne said to Jerry.

"We'll just keep trying to sell this place and get out," Jerry said as he put his arm around Suzanne's shoulders.

Suzanne went back inside. Jerry went to get the mail. When he stepped into the house, he motioned to Suzanne, "Come here, let me show you something."

Suzanne walked into the entry area. Jerry was standing with his hand behind his back. "Look what was laying on the road next to the mailbox," he said as he extended his hand and opened it. It was a two-inch-tall troll doll with pink hair that was sticking straight up. It was filthy and looked like it had been run over.

Jerry smiled and Suzanne laughed. "Yuck! Get it out of this house," Suzanne said. The look on her face was one of disgust.

Jerry laughed at her reaction and stepped out on the porch to throw the doll as far as he could out into the street. "That thing is bad luck," he said as he closed the door.

Chapter 21

Suzanne was in a meeting at work when a co-worker came and whispered to her, "Your husband is on the phone. There's an emergency at home."

Acting as calmly as possible, Suzanne eased out of her meeting room and went to the nearest phone to call home. Her palms were sweating as she dialed the number.

"What the heck's going on over there? Are you okay?" Suzanne asked with the most controlled tone of voice she could manage.

"Yes, I'm okay. But guess what happened this morning?"

"I don't know. What?" Suzanne asked with growing concern.

"Gladys' limb fell on our house," Jerry told her.

"Oh, shit. What's the damage?" Suzanne managed to say. She tried to picture what was going on at the house. She imagined the dark sky and thunderstorm with Gladys singing wildly on her porch as Jerry tried to figure out how to keep the rain out of the house. Her shoulders tightened with stress.

"Well, there's a hole in the roof. It hit right where the new upstairs bathroom is located. I've called the insurance company. They're going to send a guy out with a tarp to cover the hole. Right now, I can't tell just how much damage has been done. There's not a lot of water coming into the house yet, just a couple of trickles coming in that I can see, but it was that huge limb we've been trying to get Gladys to cut for the past six months," Jerry explained.

"Have you talked to her yet?" Suzanne asked.

"Yeah, listen to this, she ran out when it fell to see if it had fallen on <u>her</u> house. When she saw me out there, she went back inside. I saw Frank out there and told him that I had reported it to the insurance company. He didn't say much, but he nodded and said he would tell his mother," Jerry told Suzanne. "After about thirty minutes, Gladys came to the door and asked me what the expense was going to be on the house. I told her we have a $500 deductible, but beyond that, I wouldn't know until the claim adjuster comes out and give us an estimate. She said she'd pay the deductible for us."

"You've got to be kidding me. Are you serious? She's actually doing the right thing? I've heard it all now," Suzanne said incredulously. She was suspicious of Gladys' gracious turnaround. She knew that Gladys was just trying to buy her way out of trouble.

When Suzanne spoke to the claims adjuster the next day, she mentioned the letter that she'd written to Gladys regarding the limb. "Yes, please send that to me. We're going to subrogate, and we'll need a copy of the letter you sent and the certified card that she signed. Somebody's going to get out to your house today and put together an estimate," said the adjuster.

Suzanne faxed the letter and signed certified card to the adjuster. The estimate for repairs came back at $1,400. A roofing company came out and fixed the roof the following week. A few days after the repair was complete, Suzanne was in the house cooking and heard Gladys shouting at Jerry in the front yard. She turned the stove off and ran to the front porch to see what was going on. Gladys was holding a letter and angrily pointing it at Jerry as she spoke. Jerry held his hands in the air as if to say he didn't know what she was talking about and he walked into the house.

"She just got a letter from our insurance company asking her for the money to fix the roof. She's flipping out!"

"Well, she thought she was going to be smart and let that limb fall on the house. Look who's finally got to pay," Suzanne mused. "The ironic part was that it was only going to cost a hundred dollars to have the limb removed and we were going to pay for half of it." Suzanne shook her head and smiled. "That's what she gets for being a big, stupid bitch."

Suzanne's dirty language didn't even surprise her anymore. She'd never been one to curse and refer to people the way she was talking about Gladys. It seemed like the contempt Suzanne had developed while working on this house had escalated just like her resentment and dislike of her neighbor. She didn't like herself much anymore either.

Suzanne spoke to the adjuster again the next week to let her know that the roof had been repaired and thanked her for her assistance. "Have you gotten any money from our neighbor yet?" Suzanne asked, knowing what the answer would be.

"No, but we're going to get it. That woman has called and harassed me every day since she got our letter. She calls and cusses me out and hangs up on me. She even had her daughter and step-daughter call and hassle me. No, this is one lady I'm not going to let off the hook."

"Listen, as bad as you've got it, we have to live next to this person. She hated us already, and now she's just torturing us all the time. We're selling the house just to get out," Suzanne told the adjuster.

"Good luck. I hope you get out of there and find a happy place to live. Life's too short."

Selling the house was every bit as difficult as Jerry and Suzanne had imagined. They saw people pull over to read the for sale sign, and then look at Gladys' house and shake their heads. The house on the other side of them didn't help sell their house either. The couple who lived there was in the process of a divorce. They were sloppy anyway, but the divorce situation made things worse. Nobody ever seemed to be around, and the house looked deserted and unkempt. The appliances and other junk on the porch were at least partially hidden by a couple of well-placed trees.

Potential buyers who came to look at the house often asked the same questions, "Is this a safe neighborhood?" and "Who painted that house next door that awful yellow?"

A couple of young men in a Jeep were driving by the house slowly. Jerry was outside working in the yard. He waved and said, "You guys can come in and see the house if you want."

"Are you sure?" the young man driving the Jeep said as he pulled over to the curb.

"Sure, come on in." Jerry motioned to the guys to follow him.

The young men acted excited as they stepped inside to look around. They were going to a local college and were looking for a house to share that was close to the university. After touring the house, they called their parents to come look at it. When their parents got there, they took their time walking through. Suzanne could tell they liked it. They said they would get back with them soon and that they were interested in talking about it further.

After a few days, Suzanne became impatient to hear something from the boys or their parents, so she decided to call to see if they were interested in buying the house. The young man's mother told Suzanne that they had changed their minds and that they didn't want to live in that neighborhood.

Suzanne felt heartbroken and promised herself that she wouldn't get excited about any of the prospective buyers anymore. She felt let down and depressed. Who cares anyway, she thought. She cried herself to sleep that night.

One evening about a week later, someone broke into Jerry's truck in the back yard. His wallet, tool box, ball glove, and a couple of dollars sitting in his front seat were stolen. Suzanne was getting ready for work when Jerry came in from the back yard. "We got hit again," he said as he reached for the phone.

"What? What do you mean?" Suzanne asked looking hard at Jerry.

"Somebody broke into my truck last night," he said as he dialed the phone. "We ought to put the police on speed dial." He reported the theft and then called the homeowner's insurance company to report his loss. He had a surprising calmness about him.

Suzanne finished getting ready for work and sat for awhile at the kitchen table to talk to Jerry. She had a few minutes to kill before she had to leave.

"Do you think Frank did it?" she asked.

"No, I think he's too scared to come over here. I don't know who did it, but when I find out, I'm going to make them sorry," he said. He was listing his credit cards on a piece of paper so that he could call and report them as stolen. Suzanne watched him and felt helpless.

"I wonder why Butterbean didn't bark," Suzanne said.

"I guess she slept right through it."

Jerry walked with Suzanne outside. Scattered throughout the backyard and into the alley directly behind the house were some of Jerry's business cards that had fallen out of his wallet. "Assholes," Jerry said, picking his cards up off the ground. Suzanne saw some change lying on the ground that had probably come from Jerry's truck, too.

"Well, I've got to leave for work. Are you going to be okay?" Suzanne asked as she walked toward her truck.

"Yeah, I'll be okay. I've got to get in there and report those cards as stolen," he answered.

"Look," Suzanne said as she studied the back of her truck. "They tried to get into my truck, too. See? Someone tried to open the back of it." She pointed toward the spare tire rack that was broken away from the back of her truck. "Good thing it was locked."

"Well, I thought mine was locked, too. We'll just have to start parking in the front of the house. It's safer there," Jerry said.

Jerry and Suzanne must have shown the house to fifty people. They all liked the house, but none were interested enough to make an offer. One day, a realtor called Suzanne at work and told her there was a couple that wanted to see the house. Suzanne made the appointment to meet with the prospective buyers over her lunch hour. She was sure she was wasting her time, but in the back of her mind, as usual, she was saying, "What if . . ."

When Suzanne got home, she ran around the house, making sure that everything was as clean as it could be. She prayed that Gladys would stay inside her house and not come outside singing. That had kept many people from taking the house seriously in the past.

Once the house was picked up and all the lights were turned on, she sat on a chair in the living room where she could see the people pull up in the front of the house. She could also peek through the blinds at Gladys' house. "Lord, please don't let her come outside and sing or holler at anybody." Suzanne thought about the time Gladys came outside on her porch and yelled at one of the workers, "Don't you park in front of my house!" pointing her finger toward the road and looking especially nasty with her twisted up face. Nothing would run a prospective buyer off any faster. Suzanne's stomach was hurting with nerves and anticipation, the same feeling she'd had every time anyone came to see the house. Suzanne could hear Butterbean yelping from the back yard.

When the couple got to the house, Suzanne greeted them at the door and gave them a copy of the historic homes tour booklet that highlighted their home, along with several others in the neighborhood. This had become the usual greeting and had created interest right away for buyers looking for an authentically historic home.

The man and woman acted in an unusual manner, as they didn't walk through the house together. The man went upstairs and the woman went downstairs. Then, the woman went upstairs and the man went downstairs. They didn't speak as they passed each other. Neither did they speak to Suzanne when they passed her.

Their realtor, who arrived a few minutes later, stayed on her cell phone the entire time her clients were viewing the house. She seemed detached and hardly acknowledged Suzanne's presence. How rude, Suzanne thought as she waited patiently for the showing to end.

The couple didn't have any questions and left quickly. They even drove off in separate vehicles. The woman was driving a Mercedes and the man drove a high-priced utility vehicle. They're a little too yuppyish for this neighborhood, Suzanne contemplated. Their realtor thanked Suzanne and left without giving any remarks. Oh well, Suzanne thought, I won't be hearing from them.

Suzanne closed and locked the door behind her and went back to work. She felt a little let down, but the sun was shining. She listened to the radio on her way back to work and sang along to lift her mood.

Later that afternoon, on her way home from work, Suzanne's cell phone rang. It was the realtor who had showed the house to the couple earlier that day. "Hello, Suzanne. I have some interested buyers for your house." Suzanne's heart felt like it had stopped beating. "In fact, they want to make an offer."

Suzanne was so shaken she pulled to the side of the road to talk. "Okay, what do you need from me?"

The realtor asked for a copy of the property condition report to be faxed to her. Suzanne faxed it to her that night. She was afraid to get excited, but she couldn't help herself. God, please help us sell our house, Suzanne prayed.

The next day, Suzanne was instructed to pick up the offer from the realtor's office. When Suzanne read it, her heart immediately sank. The offer was too low; it wouldn't even pay off their bills if they accepted it. Suzanne called the realtor back and left a message for her. "We just can't accept this offer. I'll write in a counter offer on the contract and hopefully the buyers will go for it. We have too much invested in the house to go this low with the price."

Suzanne dropped off the counter offer at the realtor's office and went home. She didn't even feel like telling Jerry that an offer had been made. When Jerry got home from working on a neighbor's deck, she didn't tell him right away. Later that night, she finally told him about it. "I don't see anything coming from the counter offer," she said. She felt more hopeless than ever.

The next day was a Saturday. Suzanne's father had come over and they were all going out for breakfast. As they sat eating, Suzanne's cell phone rang. It was the realtor. "Suzanne, I have a question about your house, if you have a minute to talk," she said.

"I'm having a hard time hearing you. Hang on, let me go to a quiet place in the restaurant," Suzanne said as she got up from the table.

"I can call you back if you need me to," the realtor offered.

"No, no. Wait just a second." Suzanne walked to the bathroom area of the restaurant where it was quieter. "I'm sorry. Go ahead. What's your question?" She was so anxious, she felt like she couldn't breathe or else she would totally mess up and answer the question wrong. She didn't want anything to get in the way of getting the house sold.

"Can your basement be used to park a car in?" the realtor asked.

"Yes, but the opening would have to be widened," Suzanne answered. She finally exhaled and felt a little relieved. She had been afraid that the question would be about something that was so grossly wrong that it couldn't be changed.

"But a motorcycle could be parked down there, right?" the realtor asked.

"Definitely."

"Well, the buyers have accepted your counter offer. Congratulations!" the realtor said.

Suzanne thanked her and hung up the phone. She was numb and felt like she was in a daze. She went back to the table where Jerry and her father were still eating. "We just sold our house," Suzanne said. She was smiling.

"What? Are you serious?" Jerry asked.

"Really?" Paul said at the same time.

"I wouldn't lie about a thing like that!" Suzanne was grinning ear to ear. "I don't want to get overly excited, though, 'cause anything could happen and this deal could fall through. I'm scared I'll jinx it if I'm too happy about it."

Suzanne was so keyed up she couldn't finish eating. She tried to push daydreams aside of signing papers, packing boxes, and moving. In her mind, she could see herself shedding the constant worry and distress of the past two and a half years. She looked at Jerry, and he had a satisfied look on his face, though he had changed the subject and was talking about politics. Finally, their prayers had been answered – she hoped.

Chapter 22

Jerry and Suzanne only had a few weeks to get ready for the move. Suzanne had terrible thoughts about the sale of the house falling through. She lay in bed at night and worried about it, tossing and turning. Telling herself it does no good to worry, Suzanne tried to dismiss her scary thoughts by imagining her stress-free life. She envisioned sitting in a living room somewhere, anywhere, the sun streaming through the windows, and the only sound being the birds singing outside. Suzanne could feel the tension fade when her thoughts went to happier places.

Jerry and Suzanne decided to go through with their divorce. It was a difficult decision, but one that they both knew would have to be made eventually. They had no hard feelings toward each other, and after everything they'd been through together, they felt that there was no sense in arguing about anything. After the closing, Suzanne would move in with a friend and Jerry was going to move to Florida, which was what he had planned to do before they bought the house at 2010 Cumberland Street.

The decision was made to divide their belongings into separate storage areas. Elaine and Paul came to help them get ready for the move. Paul used his truck to haul things to storage, and Elaine stayed at the house with Suzanne packing boxes. There was not only a house full of furniture and other personal items, but Jerry was a packrat who never threw anything away. They gave away or sold a lot of things that had been stored in the basement.

During a break, Elaine went onto the front porch to smoke. When she came back into the house, she motioned for Suzanne to talk to her in the kitchen so no one could hear. "That boy next door just said he was going to kick my ass," she said. Suzanne wanted to laugh, but Elaine was dead serious.

"Do what?" Suzanne asked. "He said what?" Elaine's serious look made Suzanne smile.

"I was smoking on the front porch, and he said he was going to kick my ass because I'm smoking outside," Elaine answered. "Don't say anything to Jerry. Let's just get this shit out of here before there are any more problems." Elaine's eyes were wide as she spoke.

Suzanne went to the mailbox, pretending to check it for mail, and sure enough, Frank was sitting on the front porch next door, looking like he was stoned. He was slunk down in a chair gazing toward the street. Suzanne looked at the ground as she walked back to her house.

"Skeletons comin' all out of her closets!" he screamed at Suzanne as she walked back up to the house.

This was too weird. "Did you hear that?" Suzanne asked Elaine when she got back into the house.

"I couldn't understand what he was hollering at you, but I'd say we better stay away from the front of the house," Elaine said raising her eyebrows high. Suzanne laughed.

Most of the moving was taking place out of the back of the house. Suzanne went to see how everything was going with Jerry and Paul. A lot of things had been moved, but there was still a basement full of stuff to be sorted and either thrown away, or put on the moving truck.

"Didn't I tell y'all to quit making noise?" a voice said.

"What the hell?" Paul said. "Who said that?"

Next door, Frank was sitting on top of the roof, yelling at the movers and at everyone else. "Don't make me come down there and make y'all be quiet." He had a book in his hand and was grinning. Suzanne realized he was holding a Bible.

"He's flipped his lid!" Suzanne said.

Jerry said, "Just keep working, everybody. Don't pay attention to that." He was sweating profusely from working in the stagnant heat of the day, loading things out of the basement into Paul's truck.

Elaine rolled her eyes. "Like I said, let's just get this shit packed and get out of here." She went back into the house, grabbed a box and began filling it with items from a bookshelf.

Frank climbed off the roof and momentarily disappeared. Suzanne felt uneasy and worried about where he might have gone. The soon-to-be new owners were coming for their final walk-through that day before the closing, and if they saw him acting like that, it would be all over.

The couple pulled up in front of the house. Suzanne walked out on the porch, partly to greet them and also to see what was going on next door. Suzanne noticed Frank working on a lawnmower in his yard, which seemed pretty harmless for the moment. Maybe her prayers would be answered.

Suzanne kept watching out of the side window to see if things stayed calm next door. It seemed to take forever for the buyers to walk through the house. There was no air conditioning on since the back doors were wide open for moving, and the house was hot and sticky. Hurry up, people! Suzanne thought. It seemed like the buyers were in slow motion as they walked through the rooms of the house. Suzanne was sweating and felt sick.

When the walk-through of the house was complete, Suzanne didn't waste any time with small talk. "We'll see you at the closing in a couple of hours!" she said as she waved to the buyers, rushing them out, but trying to make it look like it was because she was busy packing and moving the final things out of the house.

Frank was still working on his mower next door. He had a hammer and a screwdriver in his hand. Within a few minutes after the couple pulled away, Suzanne saw Frank go back into his house and come out with a Bible. He was standing over the mower urging it to start by the order of God. Thank goodness he wasn't doing that when those people were here, Suzanne thought as she headed back into the house to finish packing.

Most everything had been moved out of the house, so everyone except Jerry and Suzanne left. "Call me when the closing is over so I know it went through," said Elaine as she got in her truck to leave.

"I will. I just hope they don't drive by here again and see that fruitcake next door acting crazy out in the yard," Suzanne said.

When Jerry and Suzanne got to the title company, they were still a little nervous that the closing wouldn't take place. What if the buyers change their mind at the last minute? What if they make an issue out of something that couldn't be changed? Jerry forced himself to be positive and thought about the time he was going to spend fishing once this whole disaster was over.

In reading the closing statement, it was evident that Jerry and Suzanne weren't making money on the deal; they were, in fact, barely breaking even. There was the cost of paying a commission to the buyers' realtor, the $10,000 prepayment penalty, and the payoff for the new heating and cooling unit that they had to purchase for the house in the beginning to replace the old broken furnace. The loan for the unit had been placed as a lien against their house. There was also a lien from another lender that resulted from a loan that they had gotten to pay off high interest credit card bills that had been accumulating for years. Of course, Jerry's parents had to be repaid as well, even though they didn't ask for money back on the food they had bought for Jerry and Suzanne. Their generosity was unbelievable.

After the closing was over, Suzanne urged Jerry to hurry and get on the elevator. She was still afraid that something could go wrong. "Hurry up. I don't want to ride the elevator with those people," she whispered.

"It's over now. The papers are signed!" Jerry said laughing.

"I know, but just in case, let's get the heck out of here."

Jerry laughed again. "Stop worrying. We've got to get to the bank and wire the money to Mom and Dad. After that, we can grab some lunch. Please smile." He faked one of his toothy grins.

"You're right. I guess I've just developed a bad habit of worrying," Suzanne said as she smiled back at him. She dialed her cell phone to let Elaine know the sale went through.

"Are you sure?" Elaine laughed. "Well, I'm happy for you. What are you going to do now?"

"You know, I'm not sure. I'll have to talk to you later about it, if you know what I mean," Suzanne said quietly as she walked away from Jerry. She tried to sound casual, as if she were talking about the weather.

"Yeah, I know. Hey, where's Butterbean?" Elaine asked.

"She's in the house. We still have to go by there and get a few more things. We laid out a towel for her to lay down on, so she's fine. As a matter of fact, the security system is on, so if anybody breaks in to bother her, it'll go off."

"Well, I'm glad she's safe," Elaine said dryly. Butterbean had tried to bite her on several occasions, and it was clear that she didn't like Butterbean. "Call me if you need anything."

Chapter 23

After the closing, Jerry and Suzanne went back to the house to collect the last of their possessions. They only had a few more items to pack, about an hour's worth of work. They worked in silence, both relieved and sad, but mostly they were just exhausted from the adrenaline rush of the closing. Suzanne felt like she'd been holding her breath all day and she could finally breathe.

Suzanne had parked her truck out front and Jerry pulled in the back of the house from the alley. The remaining things to be moved could be taken out of the back door and loaded into the back of his truck. They tied Butterbean to a big tree in the back yard and gave her food and water. She looked weary with her panting tongue hanging out.

Scanning the house for remaining belongings to be packed, Suzanne felt shaky and hot. She leaned against the stove to rest for a minute. It was humid, and she felt the sweat trickle down the side of her face. As she paused to get her bearings, it dawned on her that she never packed the pots and pans that were stored in the drawer at the bottom of the stove. She found an empty box and began stacking them in it as best they would fit.

Jerry walked in and said, "Oh, we almost walked out without our cookware." Then he thought about what he'd just said. "I mean, did you want those or do you want me to take them?" The simple question hung in the air like a sad proposal waiting to be accepted.

Suzanne couldn't look at Jerry, but instead focused on the box filled with the pots that she'd stacked as neatly as she could. "Um, well, you probably need them more than I do. Go ahead and take them." She felt the heat of emotion rise up her neck. Throughout the process of moving, they had discussed the ownership of several possessions in the house as they packed everything in bags or boxes. Until now, however, there were other people around and it was easy to act casually about it. Now they were alone, and talking about divvying up their belongings made Suzanne's heart feel like it was going to break right in half. Her throat was hoarse as she spoke, "I'm dying for something to drink. What did you do with that bottle of water you had?"

When she looked up at Jerry, she knew that he was holding back powerful feelings. It felt awkward as they stood in the hot kitchen they had worked on for so long. These were the last moments they would spend in the same house as husband and wife. Jerry handed Suzanne the bottle of water from the counter behind him and walked into the next room. It seemed almost too much to bear, this loneliness that was already washing over him.

Suzanne watched him leave the room and thought about the events that brought them to this point. She knew that her immaturity had played a considerable part in the ending of their marriage. The fact that Jerry hadn't kept a steady job was really more of an excuse than a real reason, Suzanne thought. She recognized that her own indiscretions and selfishness were to blame for a lot of the regretful things that had happened.

The house was a delusion of Suzanne's that never lived up to her unrealistic expectations. She somehow believed it would heal things between them. The thought of living life without her best friend blinded her from the reality that their marriage had been over for a long time. They weren't even intimate anymore. Again, her own selfish need to keep Jerry in her life superceded rational thought.

Letting go of Jerry, no matter how unhappy they made each other sometimes, seemed like the end of the world to Suzanne, impossible to the core of her being. Maybe it took the agonizing experience of sweating their guts out on this dilapidated old house, and all of the miserable incidents that went along with it, to finally end their marriage. Suzanne remembered a time when nothing seemed big enough to do that.

She felt foolish as she looked around at their most unfortunate attempt to keep things together. Suzanne realized that it wouldn't have mattered if anyone had tried to stand in their way, they were determined and felt unstoppable, almost defiant in the faces of those who thought they couldn't pull it off. They were downright defensive about the project in the beginning, scoffing at anyone who gave negative feedback. All of that seemed so long ago now. We sure showed them, Suzanne thought regretfully. She focused on putting tape on the box she had finished packing.

Jerry met Suzanne out on the back porch as she came back from placing the last box in his truck. "You want to take one last walk-through of the house before we lock up?" Jerry asked.

"Yes, I do," answered Suzanne.

Through the heavy humidity of the house they walked, taking a last look for any forgotten possessions they might have missed. Suzanne looked at the beautiful hardwood floors that had been one of the first projects. She remembered the battle they had to fight just to get those floors under their feet.

Jerry looked at the walls and ceilings on which he'd worked endless hours. Living in the grit, dust, exhaustion, pain and fear . . . What was it all for? Would it ever really be appreciated by anyone else? He shook his head in disbelief as the thoughts went through his mind. The torturous existence of the past two and a half years should have resulted in a lifetime home for them. Now it was just another piece of property that belonged to someone else.

After finishing their walk-through, Jerry and Suzanne stood in the house, looking at each other. "This is it, I guess," Suzanne said.

Jerry put out his hand to hold hers and said, "Yep, I guess so." It was a profound moment, one that would forever remain in their memories.

After a couple of minutes of reverence, Suzanne asked Jerry, "Can you please walk out of the house with me and I'll drive you around to the alley to pick up your truck? I'm scared to go out into the front yard by myself."

She walked to the room closest to Gladys and Frank's house and peeked out the blinds. Frank was slouched in a chair on the porch. "Asshole is sitting out there." She still felt like crying, but she laughed at her statement.

"Sure," Jerry said. He didn't seem to find the humor in what Suzanne said. "Let me put these keys on the mantel before we leave." He placed the house keys on the beautiful tiger oak mantel that had caught his attention the first day he stepped into the house.

"Oh, I better go get Butterbean," Suzanne said as she headed out the backdoor to retrieve her dog. Birds were singing, and it was turning out to be a pretty day despite the heat. As Suzanne leaned down to untie the dog, she paused for a moment to take one last good look at the back yard. She remembered when it was all torn up from the work they were doing. All the scars were healed now, and the grass had grown back where there once was only mud. The deck and covered back porch looked especially welcoming. Suzanne looked back at the house to see if Jerry was looking out the window. He wasn't. Suzanne let the dog run toward the house as she took her time walking back up the porch steps and into the house.

Heading out the front door, they were surprised to see Frank walking down the steps from his front porch. He was holding a Bible and a necklace with a large cross pendent on it. He walked to the middle of his yard and stopped. The expression on his face was blank as he looked up to the sky, his left hand thrusting the Bible toward the heavens mumbling, "Why, Jesus?"

The cottonwood tree was raining profuse amounts of soft, cottony wisps through the air, and it was as if Frank was in a snow globe, suspended in time and locked away in his own mind. He didn't even acknowledge Jerry and Suzanne walking past, his eyes staring toward the sky.

As they continued to walk down the sidewalk to get into Suzanne's truck, Gladys stepped out onto her porch, letting the screen door slam shut. She was smoking a cigarette and watching them with no reaction. She yelled "Hello!" at a passing neighbor who kept on walking without answering. Suzanne and Jerry got into the truck and they looked back at what used to be their house. Even with the tall grass in the front yard and the desperate emptiness all around, it was a handsome house.

Chapter 24

"So, how's single life?" Vergie asked as she put her arms around Suzanne. They met for lunch to visit.

Vergie smelled like cigarettes and Suzanne held her breath when they hugged. "I guess it's okay. How's everything with you?"

"Well, it's about the same. Have you heard from Jerry?" Vergie sat down in the booth at the restaurant and scooted all the way to the window.

"Yes, we stay in touch. He sounds like he's doing just fine in Florida. We talk on the phone and write letters occasionally."

They ordered some drinks and settled in to have a chat. Suzanne was strangely eager to hear about the happenings in her old neighborhood. It had been several months since she had heard anything new.

"First of all, Frank has also completely lost his marbles. He's been running around the neighborhood acting like a fool with a wild look in his eyes. The police are always out at that house, but I guess that's nothing different from when you lived there."

"No, that's not much of a surprise." Suzanne sipped her iced tea.

"There was this one time, three police cars had him cornered because somebody called the police saying they were scared of him. Said he was walking down the street with a dead squirrel in his hand. He was jabbering and acting like a nut. Somebody said that he thought he could bring the squirrel back to life. Seems to me he really started acting crazy one day when a bunch of helicopters flew over his house real low," said Vergie, as if that was a valid explanation of Frank's actions.

"Oh, brother, it's too bad you have to put up with all that silly stuff. Sometimes I think about you and your kids and wonder how you can stand living there."

"Suzanne, it's just something I'm used to now. Not too long ago, Frank told me he was gay. Maybe he feels like he can confide in me. I don't feel threatened by him or his mother. They mostly just get on my nerves."

Vergie went on to tell Suzanne that the people who had bought her house only stayed there a year and then resold it. She said that maybe they were afraid for their small children to be raised there or maybe the stress of living there was tearing their family apart just like it did with Jerry and Suzanne. "The people who live in the house now paid a bunch of money for it. They seem happy there, as far as I can tell."

Suzanne decided to take a drive through her old neighborhood when she parted ways with Vergie. The area was still improving overall, and new rehabilitation projects had begun. One particular house that had fallen into disrepair had been remodeled and turned out to be one of the grandest and most majestic homes in the neighborhood. Suzanne sat in her car in awe of the change that had taken place. She remembered that the roof was caving in and that the house had been deemed unsafe for human habitation. There had been a sticker from the Department of Human Services on the front window that said so.

Another home down the street on the corner had also been remodeled. It was updated once about a decade ago, but the second remodel project done on the home brought out the beauty that the home was destined to show. The turret on the outside of the home was topped with an impressive copper roofing material that gave it a striking appearance.

She had read in the paper that skilled craftsmen were buying the homes at a reduced rate and restoring them to beautiful conditions. It was profitable for them and beneficial for the neighborhood. The value of the homes in general was still increasing. She was glad, for her neighbors' sakes that things were improving.

Suzanne initially stayed in touch with a couple of her old neighbors when she first moved, but after several months, she didn't contact them anymore and even though they had her phone number, they didn't contact her either. It was all just as well since Suzanne had moved on to a whole new life.

Jerry spoke with a couple of neighbors pretty regularly and occasionally heard gossip from the neighborhood, which he passed along to Suzanne. Sometimes it was good for a laugh.

For a couple of years following the sale of the house and even after the divorce was final, they kept in touch and often called each other to talk about things. Suzanne had gotten remarried and Jerry had developed his own painting and home remodeling business.

Jerry called Suzanne one day on her cell phone. "Bushpig died," he said unceremoniously without saying hello or anything else.

"Are you serious?" Suzanne managed to say. She was getting ready to head out the door and stopped to listen.

"Yes, she died in October. I heard about it from Pete." Pete was one of the neighbors with whom Jerry had stayed in touch since they had left the neighborhood.

"Really?" Suzanne weighed the information that Jerry had just told her. Somehow the news didn't affect her the way she thought it would. She realized that she really didn't care. "Remember when we thought it would have been a blessing a couple of years ago?" Suzanne said.

"Yeah. You know, I feel awful about the way I hated her."

Suzanne said, "Yes, I know what you mean. I wonder what'll happen to her old house now. Is Frank going to stay there?"

"I guess. I really don't know, though. Well, I know you're in a hurry, so I'll let you go. I just thought you might want to know," Jerry told Suzanne. He said goodbye and started to hang up the phone.

"Wait, how's Butterbean?" Suzanne asked before Jerry had a chance to hang up.

"She's fine. She's a skink chaser these days. That's her job. She chases all the skinks out of the neighborhood." Jerry laughed slightly. He sounded distant.

Suzanne stalled for a few minutes, not really wanting to end the call. "That's funny. Yeah, she's a good skink chaser. I just thought I'd ask about her. Well, um, I'll talk to you later," Suzanne said. She wanted to ask him how he's really doing, but since her husband Greg was in the same room with her, she thought it was a better idea to just end the conversation.

After Suzanne got off the phone, she told her husband, "You won't believe this, but Bushpig died."

"Well, I'll be damned," Greg answered, looking surprised. He paused for a moment to think about what he'd just heard. He picked up his wallet and put it in his pocket. "Well, let's go or we're going to be late."

"What did she die of?" Greg asked over his shoulder as they made their way to the car.

"She had all kinds of things wrong with her. I guess it was probably her heart," Suzanne answered, still letting the news sink in as she followed Greg down the stairs to the garage.

"Don't you think it's ironic that she would die after you sold the house and moved out?"

"Yes, kind of. I mean, I used to wish her dead all the time. Actually, I wanted to kill her myself, but you can't just go around killing people because they're mean to you."

"Hey," Greg said as they got in the car, "you had such a tough time with that house and all those problems with the neighbors, you ought to write a story about that."

"Hmmm, you think so? Do you think anybody would want to read about something like that?" Suzanne asked dismissively with a frown. She imagined people reading it and thinking it was boring or being critical of her story, which was distressing to her. How could she possibly put her story and all of her emotions into a book for other people to scrutinize? Would they think she was a terrible person for hating a mentally ill person so badly? Wouldn't readers find it incredibly depressing?

"Oh, hell yeah, some of it's so crazy and hard to believe that people won't be able to put the book down. You ought to do it. Really. It's like a bad car wreck. You don't want to look but you just have to," Greg said.

Suzanne looked at Greg. He was such a believer in her abilities. "Greg, I don't know how to write a book. It's a hard thing to do! You have to get everything in the right chronological order and write about it in a believable way. I don't know how to do that. Besides, it'll just make Jerry and me look bad. It'll sound like we were mean to some poor old mentally ill woman or something."

"I don't know, I just think it would be a good thing to do. Even if it doesn't go anywhere, you might have fun writing it."

She thought about what he said and decided she would consider it. What did she have to lose? At least it would be good therapy for her to write it all out.

"Would you read a book called *Bushpig*?" Suzanne asked Greg with a grin.

He laughed and said, "I'd read it just to find out what the heck a Bushpig is."

"That's funny, because I don't have any idea what a Bushpig is either." Suzanne laughed, too.

Chapter 25

Several years went by before Suzanne went back to her old neighborhood to observe the progress that had taken place since she'd moved away. She hadn't been back since the day she'd met Vergie for lunch. She had purposely avoided going because of all the remaining unpleasant feelings she had about it. She felt like it was time, though, to see it again and decided to go by herself. She took the exit off the interstate and saw the rooftops of some of the houses. Almost instantly, she felt the old familiar tenseness that she had suffered from when she lived there.

As she drove down Cumberland Street, she saw Frank walking down the road by himself. When she lived there, he was always walking the roads -- usually because he had no car and needed to get somewhere and to a certain extent because he was bored. Jerry used to say Frank walked up and down the road just to get out of the house and away from his mother. Suzanne was surprised to see how fat he'd gotten. He was pretending to dribble a basketball and shoot it into an invisible hoop. He looked at her, but didn't seem to recognize her. He skipped on down the road dribbling his imaginary basketball.

Suzanne thought back to the times when he cussed her and Jerry out and tried to instigate fights. Now he looked so out of it that Suzanne seriously doubted he could hold a sensible conversation at all, much less have the courage to speak to anyone that way again. He was bigger in size, but his demeanor was one of a pathetic dim-wit. He looked like a shell of his former self. "What a stupid idiot," Suzanne said out loud to herself as she drove on past him.

She then drove to the house that she and Jerry had owned and parked for a few minutes at the curb. The house looked almost exactly as it did when they lived there, except the back yard had been fenced in and the eaves had finally been painted. That was one of the final projects that they never got around to doing. There was a rocking horse on the front porch. Suzanne hoped the child that was living there was having a good experience growing up in the old house.

It was autumn, and the leaves were blowing around in circles on the ground. Suzanne had the window down and could smell fall in the air. It was much like the day she and Jerry had found the house in the first place. Suzanne wondered if she and Jerry could have worked things out if they had not had Gladys to contend with while they were living there. She dismissed the thought almost immediately; the situation next door was a contributing factor, but not the main reason for the divorce. Suzanne refused to give that much power to the people who made her life so miserable for so long.

Suzanne turned her attention to the other house next to theirs, which had been a rental house the entire time she and Jerry lived next door to it. It was looking good in comparison to how it had appeared back then. The owners had finally put some money into it, and new renters with respect for their surroundings had moved in. The place was neat as a pin. Suzanne was glad to see it, but she was a little resentful that this major clean up effort came after they moved out. She remembered making a call to the owners, complaining that prospective buyers didn't want to live next to such a pigsty. At that time, Suzanne had gotten no response. Now they fix it up, Suzanne thought. "Hmph," she said out loud.

Gladys' house looked exactly the same, except there was no screen door at all now. Suzanne guessed it finally fell off its hinges. The place was a somber sight; it almost looked as if it were deserted. Gladys had always sat out on her porch, and it looked so different without her big body sitting on that green chair. Even the bright yellow color seemed to have muted somewhat over time.

Suzanne wondered how the bills were being paid there. While Gladys was alive, her disability and social security checks had kept the household going. Suzanne figured it was none of her business and started her car.

As she drove out of the neighborhood, she saw several kids walking down the road laughing and playing. She recognized a couple of them and waved. They waved back and kept on walking and giggling. Suzanne also saw another neighbor with whom she and Jerry had been friends while they lived there. He was walking his dog down the street and turned to see her drive past. Suzanne waved, but she felt as though he really didn't recognize her. She noticed that he watched her drive past him and down the road out of his sight.

Suzanne looked in the rearview mirror at herself. She saw a wiser lady looking back, instead of a hopeful girl full of misguided dreams. She felt so much older than she was when she first started the house project with Jerry. Her limitations seemed obvious to her now, but back then, she felt like she could take on the world. "Oh well, can't take back the past." Suzanne sighed as she looked back at the road.

Suzanne thought back to the time when they were desperate to sell their house and get out of this neighborhood. She knew she never wanted to live in, much less fix up, an old house again. The idea behind a historical neighborhood was to keep the past alive but all Suzanne wanted to do was purge the memory of an old house, a failing marriage and an ill-fated neighbor known to her and Jerry as Bushpig.

Epilogue

"That was just great," Suzanne said to Greg as she put her seatbelt on. They had just walked around downtown taking in some music and good food. It had been a beautiful day that they had shared together as a family.

"You're right, that was really fun. I guess we better get home and put the baby in bed," Greg said as he pulled out of the parking garage.

Suzanne glanced at the baby sitting in his car seat. He was already rubbing his eyes with tired frustration. Suzanne smiled at him and reached back to pull the hood of his jacket away from his face. What a pretty little baby, she thought with pride.

Greg started the car and headed toward home. "It was good to get out of the house today."

"Yes, it was. Sometimes it's just nice to walk around downtown. I think we wore our little guy out."

Greg laughed softly. "Yeah, maybe he'll sleep all night now."

"Can we drive past my old house?" Suzanne said suddenly. "The baby's asleep, and it's on our way home. Please?"

"Sure. Which way is it again?"

Suzanne directed Greg to the house. She knew he'd recognize how to get there once he saw the streets, but she had to admit, it had been so many years since she'd been through the old neighborhood, she was a little sketchy on the directions from downtown.

When they finally reached the street where the house stood, everything looked pretty much the same as it did the last time she drove through the neighborhood. As they approached Suzanne's previous home, they immediately noticed that Gladys' house had been repainted. Then they were surprised to see that it had been completely remodeled on the outside.

"Hold on a minute!" Suzanne whispered loudly. "Holy shit! Look at Gladys' old place. Look! It's been redone. Pull over; I've got to see this!"

"Yeah, you're right. Wow. That's unbelievable."

"This is amazing." Suzanne and Greg looked at each other in astonishment. "I'm going to get out and look through the windows. The curiosity is killing me."

Suzanne opened the car door as quietly as possible and stepped out into the evening air. She noticed that there was a for sale sign in the front yard. I wonder what happened to Frank, Suzanne thought as she walked toward the front door of Gladys' old house. Many feelings came rushing toward her as she stepped up onto the front steps. Everything looked so nice. Gone was the hideous yellow color, replaced by a muted, soft grey color of paint. The front porch was new and had a wooden railing all the way around it.

The front door had windows of beveled glass and a shiny brass knocker. Suzanne timidly peeked in the front window. She was almost afraid someone would catch her, or that Gladys herself would come barreling through the front door at her. Inside she saw beautiful hardwood floors, built-in bookcases and delicate-looking fixtures mounted on the ceilings and walls. She couldn't see very far into the house as evening was closing in on her. She strained to see more, but the way the shotgun house was built would only allow her to see into the first couple of rooms. It was obvious that someone had spent big bucks to remodel this house.

She headed down the concrete walkway back to the car. She could see her husband looking at her and her sweet baby asleep in the backseat. For a moment, she felt like she'd gone back in time while looking into Gladys' house. She was grateful that she'd gotten past that period of unhappiness and had moved on to a better life. Her footsteps felt light as she descended the front steps down to the sidewalk.

"What did you think?" Greg asked as Suzanne got back into the car.

"As far as I could tell, the inside of the house has been redone, too. It's just unbelievable." Suzanne didn't say much more on the way home. She looked at the remaining light from the sunset and knew that it would be gone in minutes. She realized that she was never meant to be content in that old house. She also knew that she and Jerry weren't meant to be together. Too many forces were working against them.

As Suzanne thought about her small family, she knew that she was exactly where she belonged. She wondered if it was fate or the good Lord who led her to where she was now. All she knew for sure was that she had what she'd really always wanted in the first place -- a family, a home, and an inner peace that comes from knowing that when things are meant to be, they will happen in their own good time.

About the Author

Carol Preston lives in Middle Tennessee with her husband and son. Her career path has been working in Human Resources for several years. She also has a realtor's license and occasionally "pretends" to sell real estate on the side.

However, Carol readily admits that her passion is writing and, as an expressive medium, writing is also her therapeutic pastime.

Otherwise, you might find Carol spending time with her family – playing with her young son, biking, or looking for her next writing adventure.